M000045767

Love, Limitations, and Motives

Author, Deitra L. Tucker
Editor, Joseph Editorial Services, LLC
Book cover by, Dion Lynk

ACKNOWLEDGMENTS

The life lessons we go through and learn serve as a testimony. In writing this book, I received true healing that only God can give. Without Him, this book would not be possible.

What I learned from this journey is to love myself first. Ladies and gentlemen, please practice this daily because the more you love yourselves, the more you want the best for you without settling for less.

To my children, Missy, Ronnie and Tony Thank you for believing in me and rooting me on. To my grandchildren I love each and every one of you!

T.L. Tucker you are my inspiration, never put your pen down.

Tikkia {Poetic Relief} Wills you are one of the best editors I know. Thanks for believing in me as well as giving me your expertise.

I dedicate this book to my best friend and mother Francenia E. Tucker
I miss and love you very much Mom. Thank you for your gift of writing.
"Deedawee"

PROLOGUE

Stunned, Dana sat in the chair beside the phone trying to get her thoughts together. *Nate did not show up for work today?* She reached for the phone and dialed Nate's number. His phone rang four times before it went to voicemail.

She made herself a glass of wine, her mind racing as she tried to think positively, pushing aside worry and fury. She struggled to make sense of it all while questions flew through her mind. *What could have gone wrong? Why had he lied to her? Where the hell was he? Why was he not picking up his phone?* She needed answers.

Dana wasn't sure how much time had passed before she'd heard the key in the door at twelve o'clock in the morning, and she seethed at the thought.

Nate walked in and stopped when he saw her sitting in the chair by the phone. He had not expected her to be downstairs waiting for him. He tried to change his expression, but it was too late, she'd already caught it.

CHAPTER ONE

Staring out of the window, Dana thought about the day she met Nate. She remembered it like it was yesterday. She allowed herself to travel down memory lane, smiling as the sun shone bright and beautiful.

Dana and Nate met while she was having lunch with a friend. He'd made a great first impression on her. Initially she'd been surprised by the way he approached them with a corny pick up line, but he'd redeemed himself with his conversation, then he'd brought lunch for them.

His conversation had her smiling, laughing, and made her feel that she was actually a part of that situation he spoke of. She remembered the smell of his cologne, Dior for men made her mouth water. He smelled so good it was distracting.

Nate was a college graduate, he worked as a contractor for a lumber business. His beautiful brown eyes would sparkle as he smiled, and he was tall with a body that made her imagine being picked up and carried around the room. As Nate continued to speak during that first meeting, Dana noticed he did not take his eyes off of her, not even once. He spoke with such confidence and passion that it captivated her. She found that very refreshing.

Dana remembered their first date when Nate took her to Ray's in the City, a restaurant on Peachtree Street. It was one of the best times she'd ever had. They'd talked, laughed, eaten, had a couple drinks, and listened to the sultry sounds of jazz played on the piano in the dimly lit restaurant.

Periodically, Nate would take her hand and kiss it gently. She could feel the warmth of his breath as he planted tiny, sensual kisses from her hand to her neck. He was truly romantic. Dana remembered that he'd slipped the waitress money and requested the pianist to play "Fall for You," one of her favorite songs. Dana felt like she was on a cloud while she listened to the soft and sultry music of Leela James, played by the pianist. As Dana looked around the room, she felt like she could get used to having Nate by her side and knew they could have something special.

As she continued to reminisce, Dana thought about how much she'd liked the relationship she and Nate had. It was full of love and excitement. Like any new relationship, there was conversation and a lot of fun. They went many places together, including Centennial park where they rode the horse and carriage. They'd also gone riding in the country to have picnics and attended festivals. In the beginning, things were great! They were always together taking long walks, laughing, and sharing long nights of vigorous love making.

They'd been dating six months before Nate popped the question. A little quick for some, but Dana believed that when she felt good about something, she should go with it and give it a chance. They were adults and knew what they wanted, so Dana said yes. She didn't think of how things could turn out due to her hasty decision. She believed that she and Nate were in love and nothing could change that.

"I Nate, take you Dana as my lawfully wedded wife," he repeated as he slipped the ring around her finger, looking deeply in her eyes. He smiled at her as he watched her eyes sparkle with love and tears.

They'd decided to go downtown to the Justice of the Peace, since neither of them wanted a big wedding nor the fuss that preceded one.

"I now pronounce you man and wife," the officiant said, as he ended the ceremony.

Nate kissed Dana with so much passion that it set something on fire inside of her. After breaking their intense embrace, they signed the papers solidifying their union and headed to the car.

Downtown Atlanta is always congested with traffic, Diana thought as they headed to the West End to his mother, Mildred's house to give her the news.

Dana had visited his mother on several occasions. She was a stocky older woman who looked like she may have been fairly nice looking in her younger days. She was a bit rough around the edges, and every time they went over there, she was either drunk, rolling or both. Once, they'd walked in on her butt naked sprawled out on the couch. Nate was visibly disturbed seeing his mother in that condition. He'd covered her up and apologized to Dana for witnessing her like that.

Dana believed his mother's strange behavior was the reason he never wanted to visit her, and when he did, he rarely took her with him. She never questioned him though. Honestly, she was relieved that she didn't have to go with him. She knew his mother didn't care for her, though she didn't know nor care why. Regardless of that, Mildred was always glad to see her only son come over.

Dana could not remember a time when Mildred was sober. Even if she was, she still gave the impression that she was high on something.

When they arrived at her house, Mildred had company there with her. It was an older woman who looked to be middle aged with salt and pepper hair and masculine features.

When Dana spoke to the other woman, she'd looked her up and down, given her a dirty look, and rolled her eyes like Dana owed her something. Dana looked back at the woman but brushed it off as if nothing happened. Both older women could have been rolling for all Dana knew, yet this was her day. She was not going to let ghetto number one and two spoil it.

"Well, well, if it isn't the happy couple," Mildred snickered to the other woman. Dana noticed the tone in her mother-in-law's voice. She also noticed the sideway glances they made at each other. The way Mildred's friend looked at her with hatred in her eyes made her feel a certain way because they didn't know one another. She also noticed how the two women kept eyeing her and Nate with snake-like grins on their faces. Dana didn't understand what was going on, but still she left it alone.

The rest of the day went by in a blur. People from the neighborhood came in and out, many of them Dana had never met. There were so many names she couldn't remember who was who, and she didn't think it mattered since she was rarely there anyway.

The day continued with congratulations and drinking. It was seven p.m. when she realized that she nor Nate hadn't eaten anything. Dana's stomach was growling so she knew it was time to eat.

It had also just occurred to her that she was no longer Dana Butler, but Mrs. Dana Johnson. She thought about it for a minute, then blushed. *Had she really done this?* She was now a married woman.

She looked over at Nate, who was talking with a few guys and their eyes met. He smiled at her and winked, then cut the conversation short and walked over to his wife to stand by her side.

Nate kissed Dana as if she were his last supper, then whispered in her ear what he was going to do to her when they were alone. Thinking of all the delicious things she would be doing later on made Dana's insides quiver with anticipation. She was ready for whatever Nate had in store for her.

The rest of the day went by quickly, leaving her little time to ponder the fact that this was the beginning of their life together as husband and wife, though she didn't feel any different now than when she awoke this morning. She'd felt that he was her husband before the piece of paper. Nate had been a part of her from the beginning. They were inseparable. Nate was all about her, all about *them*.

Later that evening, she heard someone calling out Nate's name. She looked up just in time to see him getting out of a red Ford Explorer. The woman who looked at her so strangely earlier was on the driver's side and she did not look happy. She looked over at Dana with hatred as she did earlier that evening, rolled her eyes, then she drove off.

Feeling a bit pissed and disrespected Dana said, "Okay that's it," aloud to herself. "What's up with this woman and why does she keep giving me dirty looks?"

It struck her as odd that he got out of the woman's truck, since she hadn't noticed him leave or know that he was gone. She would have to ask him about it later.

When he approached her, Dana was opening her mouth to form the question, but Nate put his arm around her and planted a kiss that took her breath away and made her body go limp. Nate looked into Dana's eyes like nothing else in the world mattered. So, she let it go as nothing because the way he looked at her said there was nothing to worry about.

Dana was handed a wine glass by a smiling

Mildred. "A toast, to the one who got him and the many who let him get away," she said with a smirk on her face. Dana looked over at Mildred as Nate approached her, and the next words out of her mother-in-law's mouth shocked her. "Girl, sometimes it is better to want than to have."

Before Dana could comment, Nate had swooped her up into his arms and was saying bye to his mother at the same time. They were in the car and riding down the street in a matter of seconds.

Dana thought about what her mother-in-law said before Nate rushed her out of the house. *What did she mean by that statement she made?*

Nate saw that Dana was in deep thought, so he broke the silence. "Are you hungry Mrs. Johnson?" he asked her.

She just looked at him. The way he said it, the way it sounded, made her feel warm inside.

"Take off your panties," Nate told her as he watched her fidget for a moment, his eyes dark with lust. Dana looked at him surprised, yet nervous for a brief moment before she complied. Before they could get out of the car, Nate had Dana's panties in his hands, putting them in his pocket. He made her face him, legs wide opened as he teased her little lady button. He fingered her all the way to their house, sending her body into a frenzy and made her cream all over herself.

Excited and out of breath, Dana could not wait to get him in their king-size bed and ride the thick piece of meat between his legs. Her mouth watered at the thought of running her tongue up and down his brown shaft, sending his body into tremors as she sucked him with hunger.

As soon as they got in the house, they stripped each other naked. Nate picked Dana up and laid her on the bottom step, then went down on her slowly, making her body jerk and spasm until she thought she could not take it anymore. He then picked her limp body up and took her upstairs to their bed where he made love to her with such fury Dana was not sure if she would be able to walk right for a week.

They fell asleep in each other's arms and juices. Dana did not mind a bit.

She woke the next morning around seven a.m., her stomach growling. She was starving. She looked around to see if her husband was there in the room with her. She giggled as she thought about how that sounded. He was her husband now and he had left the house already.

When the phone rang Dana answered. "Hello?"

"Good morning beautiful. I left for work already so I could get an early start. I also made you some coffee. Thank you for that beautiful piece of work you gave me last night. I should have married you long time ago. Being married sure has its privileges." They both laughed at that.

"Thank you, my wonderful husband," she replied, as she thought about their night of blissful lovemaking. "And ditto."

"I won't be home until late. I have a meeting today," he told her.

"So do I," Dana replied. "I have to get the

upcoming promotions out. The new brochures for the restaurant are coming out today and I need to have a meeting with the staff."

"Okay, then I'll see you later on tonight baby love," Nate responded.

"I'll talk to you soon my sexy and loving husband," Dana told him before hanging up the phone with a satisfied look on her face.

CHAPTER TWO

Dana took her shower, got dressed, made herself a cup of coffee, then left the house by 8:45. While in the car she thought about the night before and how sore she was now. *If walls could talk, the things they'd tell,* she thought with a giggle.

Business was booming at D's Bistro where she worked. She looked back a year ago and found herself in awe at how good things turned out. When she came here, the diner was going into bankruptcy, but since she'd taken over, they'd expanded to three locations. Talk about a success story.

Dana had not been this busy in a long time, so much had to be done before the new promotion started. The meeting was a success, and everybody was in agreement on how things were to be done. Being on the same page was very important to her and to the business. The owners liked her ideas and trusted her wholeheartedly; they backed her in all her decisions and negotiations. She'd made them a lot of money in just a short period of time and they'd franchised because of it.

It was now eight p.m. and she was on the way home. Pleased with herself and how good things turned out today, she stopped to get a bottle of wine to relax with. Not knowing if Nate made it home yet, she decided to get two bottles. It was Friday night and she and her new husband had the weekend off.

As she walked up to the door, she could hear jazz playing and something smelled really good coming through the cracks of the door. Nate was cooking and she had to see what it was. She opened the door and looked around. There were rose petals on the floor, and she heard humming coming from the kitchen. Dana closed the door behind her and continued through to the living room where she noticed two dozen roses in two different vases sitting on the coffee table. She smiled to herself. Just then, Nate came in to greet her.

"How was your day beautiful?" he asked, taking the bag she was carrying out of her hands. He sat it on the table, wrapped his arms around his wife and kissed her long and slow. Dana feeling the dizzying effect of it and couldn't contain her giggles. She was happy and thought she could get use to this kind of life fast.

Nate took the wine out of the bag and opened a bottle, then poured them both a glass while she walked over to where he was and stood beside the man who was now her husband.

"A toast to the sexiest woman alive."

Dana blushed as she listened to Nate give his toast, then she smiled at him and responded, "I agree."

They both laughed before he took her hand and led her to the kitchen.

The table was set beautifully, the food smelled great and she was hungry. She was surprised that she hadn't known Nate had it in him to do this. If she didn't know any better, she would have thought he paid someone to come in and do all of this. They sat down to eat, and everything was good. The spinach salad with avocados and almonds was delicious, the Cornish hens with cornbread and cranberry dressing tasted awesome. Dana was impressed and pleased that Nate went all out for her. No one had ever done that for her.

They talked about their day at work and how the guys teased him about being married. Afterwards, they sat in the living room snuggled together and listened to music as they finished off the rest of the wine. Dana offered to help Nate with the dishes, but he refused.

"Why don't you go upstairs and get ready for your husband?" he suggested instead, making Dana an offer she couldn't refuse.

With a smile on her face, she did indeed take him up on his offer. Feeling bubbly with joy, she noticed that the rose petals continued up the stairs and straight into the bedroom. They were even on the bed, in the bathroom, and in the bathtub. As she ran hot water to warm the bath and bubbles in the tub, she thought, *yes, she could definitely get used to this.*

She was relaxing in the tub thinking about everything that happened in the last twenty-four hours when she heard Nate walking up the stairs. She could hear glasses tinkling together and knew he had brought more to drink with him. Already feeling lightheaded from the first bottle, she thought

what the heck, no work for the rest of the weekend.
She could hear him pouring the liquid into the glasses. Then, he turned the intercom on to reflect the music coming from downstairs. Dana had always loved the sultry sounds of Jazz. They made her feel relaxed, romantic and sexy.

"Hey, did you miss me?" Nate asked, breaking through Dana's thoughts.

She looked up at him and smiled. "What do you think?" she asked?

"Hmm, let me see," he responded. Just then, he got down on his knees, handed her a glass of wine and told her to take a sip. As she did so, he put his hand in the warm, bubbly water and caressed her legs one at a time before reaching the center of her love spot.

Dana whimpered as she felt her whole-body melt in the hot liquid where she'd been soaking. He caressed her and teased her until she couldn't stand it anymore, then he stopped, got up where he had been kneeling and left the bathroom. Dana wondered why he had stopped, but quickly realized why when he walked back in the bathroom without a stitch of clothing on.

He picked her up out of the tub and sat her on top of the sink. Dana felt a chill go through her as she anticipated what was coming next. He came up close to her, putting his arms around her and kissed her. Holding her close, he entered her. Dana could feel her heart pump faster as heat went through her body like a lightning bolt. Dana began to sigh as Nate went in and out of her, first slow, gradually increasing speed so that Dana could not contain the shudders that went through her body. Each pump getting more vigorous and intense until Dana could not take it anymore and let out a scream.

Dana's body went limp and she breathed ragged from the sheer pleasure of it all. Nate picked her up and carried her to the bedroom, there he had already had a towel waiting for her.

Smiling to herself, she thought of how Nate had planned this night. He dried her off and handed her his glass of wine.

"Relax," he told her as he walked into the bathroom and came out with her glass in his hand. She sat back on the settee, calming her senses as she sipped the pink liquid. Moscato was one of her favorites.

"Nate is this what honeymooning feels like?" she asked him.

He looked at her and smiled. "I've never been on one, but I would think this is close."

The rest of weekend was spent with no interruptions. They created a routine; lovemaking, sleeping, and then starting over. This went on for a couple of months, and even though they had to get up for work, they always resumed back to what they had started during that weekend. Dana was happy and feeling positive about her new life.

"Dear Heavenly Father, I want to thank you for this time in my life. For now, I know what contentment is. Thank you for my husband and help me to know how to be a good wife. Let my husband

love me like Christ loves the church and help us to live by your ways, giving you the glory. Amen."

CHAPTER THREE

Into the second month of their marriage, Dana and Nate both were busy on their jobs. The marketing for the promotion on Dana's job had her working longer hours than usual that left her tired. Nate didn't mind it because he too was busy with his work. If he didn't beat her home, she was either sleep when he got there, or he was. He would always be gone by time Dana woke up, so they would catch each other by phone during the day.

Dana had been feeling peculiar all day. She couldn't put her finger on it, but something about today made her feel this way. As she put her key in the door at home, the house phone rang. She raced to open the door so she could answer it, but the answering machine beat her to it.

"Hello, Nate this is Turner. Mr. Wright was fuming today because you did not show up to work, you missed the meeting. Call me when you get this."

Stunned, Dana sat in the chair beside the phone trying to get her thoughts together. *He didn't show up for work today?* Dana reached for the phone and dialed Nate's number. His phone rang four times before it went to voice mail.

Stunned, Dana sat in the chair beside the phone trying to get her thoughts together. *Nate did not show up for work today?* She reached for the phone and dialed Nate's number. His phone rang four times before it went to voicemail.

She made herself a glass of wine, her mind racing as she tried to think positively, pushing aside worry and fury. She struggled to make sense of it all while questions flew through her mind. *What could have gone wrong? Why had he lied to her? Where the hell was he? Why was he not picking up his phone?* She needed answers.

Dana wasn't sure how much time had passed before she'd heard the key in the door at twelve o'clock in the morning, and she seethed at the thought.

Nate walked in and stopped when he saw her sitting in the chair by the phone. He had not expected her to be downstairs waiting for him. He tried to change his expression, but it was too late, she'd already caught it.

"How was work?" she asked.

He straightened up put a smile on his face and acted like nothing ever happened. "Great, I had a good day. Busy, very busy. Oh! Sorry I didn't answer your call earlier, I was in a meeting."

"Oh, really? Your job called you; they left you a message on the machine. I think you should listen to it."

Nate looked at her with a puzzled look on his face before going to the answering machine and turning it on. As the message from earlier repeated itself, Dana looked at Nate. His eyes narrowed as he listened to it. When it was finished, he looked up and at Dana accusingly. Before she could say anything, she heard glass breaking, then a moment of silence fell through the house. The television was no longer on because he had pushed it on the floor.

Then in a sudden rage Nate spoke, "So, what, just because my job called, I'm a liar?" he yelled.

"Who called you a liar?" Dana asked him calmly. "I just told you to listen to your message on the machine."

Nate looked at her but could not say a word.

"Why would your job call and say you were not at work if you were? And if you weren't at work, where were you?"

He hurled the bottle of wine at her. Dana gasped and ducked the bottle. Stunned and surprised at how things were going, she stood there in amazement. She didn't have time to move when he charged her. His hands were around her neck before she had time to think about what was happening.

Nate growled, "I am a grown ass man! My mother does not live here, and I don't have to answer any questions I don't want to!" he said while shaking her, his hands still wrapped around her neck.

Dana could not breathe because he was choking her. She clawed and scratched, struggling to get away from him. Angry that she was fighting back, he balled his fist up and swung, but she got loose from him before the hit connected.

He grabbed her by the hair and jerked her back, slapping her in the face and hitting her head up against the wall. He went on ranting like a mad man. "What was I supposed to do when I heard the message Dana? Explain myself like a child? No, I did not go to work today, and so what? If I don't show up for work, that's my business! If I choose to be out until midnight again, that's my business! If I want to have sex with someone, I will do it! You don't tell me what to do! I will do what I want to do, when I want to do it you bitch!"

He slammed her on the floor so hard it knocked the wind out of her. Dana lay on the floor until she got her breath back then she looked at Nate and asked, "Who said anything about fucking Nate?" She cried out as she tried to focus on his image.

Dazed she laid there for a minute, tears streaming down her eyes from everything that was happening. She tried to get up off the floor, but he pushed her back down.

All she could think in that moment was this was the man that she'd said "I do" to four weeks ago. Now he was abusing her because he lied to her about going to work.

Dana was getting up off the floor when he hit her in the face with something that felt like more than a hand. It was his fist and she did not see it coming. Dana laid on the floor blurry eyed, gasping for breath and trying to shake his hit off of her. *How could this man repeat vows to her when he did not mean any of them? How could this be happening to her? How could she have been so stupid?*

He looked at her for a long moment before

letting her go.

She looked at him then around at the broken glass and TV screen and thought about her broken dreams.

Nate was standing beside her at first, then he walked across the room. She could not read his face, so she kept quiet. She got up off the floor, still a little dizzy, so she held onto the wall to keep her balance. Then she turned to go upstairs. She was still crying.

"Where do you think you're going?" he asked.

She looked at him but said nothing. He walked over to her, grabbed her and turned her around to him, then asked her again.

With tears still in her eyes and rolling down her face, she looked at him and still said nothing. All of a sudden, there was a sharp pain in her stomach. She was left lying on the floor, wincing and gasping for air. He kicked her in the stomach.

"Get this shit off of the floor before I kill you!" he told her in a deep, sadistic voice. "And hurry up!"

Dana, still trying to breathe, nodded her head in obedience.

Shaken, Dana did as she was told, not believing the horror movie that had just taken place in her home so soon after they were married.

She cleaned up the mess that he made, drank a glass of wine then poured herself another. She went upstairs baffled, hurt, humiliated, betrayed and in pain due to the turn of events tonight.

Dana was in the shower, letting the hot water

run over her body and her emotions when Nate asked her what was taking her so long. His voice startled her. She thought she was alone. He had been standing there watching her for a while before he said anything.

"I'm finishing up," she answered him.

Still shaking, she turned off the water. She would never forget the look on his face as she stepped out of the shower. She dried herself with the towel hanging beside the bathtub. Dana looked up at Nate as he watched her. Was he smirking while he was watching her? No, he was actually laughing in her face, laughing at *her*.

You think you have all the sense in the world, don't you? You thought that just because I married you, I would stop being me, that I would just live behind a picket fence and be true to you," he sneered. "I'll never do that. I'm going to be true to me if I'm never true to anyone else and if I want to have female friends, that's what I am going to do. If I want to have sex with them, then I'll do that too. You on the other hand, will do what I tell you. And if I think that you're even looking at anyone else I will make your life a living hell!"

Dana shook at the tone of his voice, he sounded like the snake he really was. Why had she not thought this through? Why had she married this man knowing she knew nothing about him? Tears ran down her face. She loved him and she thought he loved her too, but he did not.

She had grown up seeing her mother go through abuse with her father. She knew she could not do the same; not now, not ever. She also knew that she could not live like this. She had to do something. He looked at her as if he was reading her mind. His eyes narrowed and he yanked Dana by the arm and pushed her into the bedroom.

The room was quiet, there was nothing but the quiet wheezing of his breath. She protested at first but then he said to her in a low ragged breath, "Dana, I love you and I'm sorry. I never want to hurt you and I'm sorry for hitting you. I never want to lose you. Please say you forgive me."

Tears ran down Dana's face. She could not believe the words coming from Nate's mouth as he rubbed and caressed her bruised body. She could not believe that the man lying on top of her would hurt her and then act as if it was that easy for her to forget. She couldn't just forget what happened. She couldn't forget how he beat her and hurt her heart.

The truth was, she did still love Nate and when she vowed *till death do us part*, she meant it in the sight of God.

Nate had abused her, violated her, had sex with her and apologized all at the same time. She didn't know what to feel. So much was going through her mind and her heart, not to mention what he was doing to her with his tongue. The truth was, at that moment, she did forgive him.

"Father God, please protect me and guide me. I'm confused and I'm brokenhearted. I need you right now. Amen!"

CHAPTER FOUR

Dana's mind raced back and forth at what happened that night. Everything seemed to be a blur. She looked over at him and thought, *how could he lay beside me so peacefully when he's betrayed me, abused me, and then licked and kissed my body like nothing went on?*

Dana's thoughts drifted to a time where feeling all alone was the last thing she ever wanted to feel. Not having anyone in her life who she could trust made her feel hopeless. This reminded her of days past, so long ago when innocence was taken and nothing in the world was ever the same again.

Had she known then what she knew now, would she have still married this man? Was she so blinded by love that she did not want to see the true man underneath? At that moment she heard his mother say, *"It is better wanting than having,"* and Dana finally understood what that meant.

She had to get her mind intact. The fact of the matter was, she was still in love with this man. He had hurt her physically, mentally and emotionally and she had forgiven him for it.

Dana lay beside Nate, wondering to herself if she could put this night behind her and go on with her life with the man she married.

Nate must have felt her thoughts because he

rolled over and pulled her to him so close, she could hardly breathe. When she moved a little trying to make herself more comfortable, he tightened his grip around her like she was trying to get away.

Dana sighed. She was tired and sore and just wanted to get some sleep. She laid there trying not to think of anything, but it was hard.

Anger started to swell up in her throat and a desperate feeling of loneliness came with it. Uncontrollable tears flowed rapidly from her eyes. Dana tried to keep from moving so Nate would not wake up. She monitored the way she breathed so it would appear that she was sleeping. Dana fought back the screams and sobs in her head so they would not come forth. Dana's heart shattered as she did the best she could to keep the woman she was from dying.

She could feel her eyes getting heavy until finally she was out for the count. She woke the next morning in bed alone.

It was hard for her to move. She felt as if she was ran over by a bus. Dana got up, went into the bathroom and she looked at herself in the mirror. There was a bruise on her face. She looked long and hard at the purplish color protruding from her cheek. The puffiness of her eyes and face made it evident that she had been hit.

She could not keep in check the pain and betrayal she felt. She said she forgave him, but she wanted answers, she needed answers and all she had was a void of nothing. She could hear music coming from downstairs and the smell of breakfast cooking. She thought she had been there all alone.

She took a deep breath, held her composure and went downstairs; Nate was there in the kitchen.

"Good morning," he said as he walked up to her, put his arms around her waist and kissed the bruise on her face. Then he kissed her on the lips. It surprised Dana, but she did not protest.

The kiss was slow and teasing. He squeezed her buttocks then slipped her gown off of her in the middle of the kitchen floor. He made love to her on the floor as if they had not a care in the world, as if he had not asked her for forgiveness for anything at all.

Afterwards, they sat at the table and ate the food he had cooked. Both of them ate in silence and didn't acknowledge each other except for the occasional glance at one another. It was Nate who broke the silence first.

"I think we should go away for a couple of days."

Dana looked surprised. That was the last thing she expected to hear from Nate. She expected to talk about the night before but not this.

"I want us to start over by having a honeymoon. Just the two of us getting away for a couple of days will make things better."

Dana heard Nate but did not know what to say. She wanted to tell him how she felt; she wanted to talk about it never happening again.

The look on Nate's face stopped her thought. Dana nodded, "Okay, but we do need to talk." She could see the wrinkle lines in his forehead as he blew out a long-drawn breath.

"I thought you said you forgive me."

She nodded yes.

"So, what is there to talk about? I told you I was sorry and that should be that."

Dana could hear the tension in his voice and decided to leave the matter alone.

"Sure, that sounds good," Dana responded.

Nate reached over to where Dana was sitting and kissed her on the forehead. He told her he had some things to take care of before they left and to be ready when he returned.

Dana got on the phone and called her job to let them know she would not be in that day. Of course, the staff were all concerned. She'd never taken a day off since she'd been working with them. Other than her wedding day and the day after, she returned to work as usual. The owners reassured her that all was well and to take as many days needed. They needed her well when she came back. She was, after all, their right hand.

Dana had the bags packed by the time Nate returned. He looked as if there was something on his mind. He grabbed the luggage and walked past her, almost bumping into her. Dana sucked her breath in. Nate heard her and with a turn, dropped the luggage and reached out for her. They looked into each other's eyes and she assured him that she was okay. He kissed her and then they walked out the door.

The ride in the car was a quiet one, as the soft sounds of Maxwell played on the radio. Dana reflected on the events that happened up to this point and it was hard not to be angry. She turned her head to look out of the window. Did he not know that it was going to take a lot more than a couple of days in a cabin to make her feel like she could trust him again? She would give him the benefit of the doubt now, but he better make it good.

They drove for a couple of hours until they came to a beautiful resort, not at all what she thought it would be, but much more. Just then, Nate broke in her thoughts, "Is it to your liking?"

She turned to look at him and answered, "So far it's beautiful. I didn't think resort when you said cabin. This place seems quite nice."

Nate looked her in the eyes, not quite feeling her energy. He knew he screwed up in a big way, but he also knew that he would never let her go. That was not an option.

As Dana walked in the cabin, she looked around in awe. This place was magnificent. Beautiful high ceilings and windows were everywhere. There was a private pool and lakefront she noticed as she walked around. She also noticed the rose petals in a trail on the floor, but she did not want to acknowledge them because she saw him watching her. She didn't want to give him anything to think he had won her over so quickly. Just then, he walked up behind her with a glass of champagne.

"Are you hungry?" he asked, handing her the glass.

She stepped away from him to continue to walk

around. "Yes, that sounds good," Dana answered him still not looking his way.

"I've noticed you walked around the whole cabin, but you have not been in the bedroom."

She turned to him with a neutral look on her face. "What could that bedroom have that ours doesn't?"

He smiled at her knowing that she was still holding a grudge for what happened. "Dana, I thought we were going to spend these days honeymooning," he said. "I thought we were starting over."

He walked up to her, placing his hand on her arm and pulling her towards him.

"We can only go from here Nate. Starting over is something different. Now can we go to dinner? I'm hungry."

"So am I," he looked her deeply in her eyes and kissed her.

Dana took in the scent of his cologne and the champagne on his breath as he skillfully teased her top lip then her bottom. She put her hand on his chest, but the kiss deepened.

"I love you Dana,' Nate said. "We are going to make this work."

He picked her up, still kissing her and walking her to the bedroom. Dana tried to protest, but Nate stopped and asked, "Do you love me?" When she didn't respond, he asked her again, "Do you love me?"

With tears in her eyes she said, "Yes."

"Then try again."

Dana shook her head yes, then he took her to the bedroom. The bedroom had been made ready with rose petals on the floor, candles everywhere, bottles of wine on ice and just outside of their window she saw the pool she'd spotted earlier. She looked down at Nate thinking of how much detail he gave this and thought if he could do it, so could she.

The next couple of days Nate made sure that Dana did not want or need anything but him and his undivided attention. They stayed in a cabin most of the time enjoying one another in the pool or jacuzzi or shopping. Nate went back to being the man she fell in love with and the days were filled with fun and laughter as the nights were filled with hot, steaming, exhausting sex.

No matter what was going on in their lives, Nate had a way of making her forget things, just by making love to her.

It made her think of the many women out there who tell you what they will and will not take from their man, but then you find out that they are going through abuse, drugs and God knows what else.

Some will say it's because they do not want to be alone, others will say it's because they really love their man, but nine times out of ten it's the sex. Dana loved Nate and the head was banging, the sex was great she admitted, but not worth dying for. Sometimes, the only way a woman can feel love or emotions from the man she's with is through sex.

It gives her something to hold on to. At least that's what she thought.

Dana never called those women stupid. She

sympathized with them in a lot of ways. She knew females that went through that type of lifestyle, but she never understood what kept them there.

Dana knew she loved Nate and she wanted her marriage to work.

I mean it's supposed to be until death do you part, right? she thought.

She had seen her mother go through things with her father that made her sick to her stomach and they were still together, had been for almost fifty years. Dana thought, *if they could stay married for fifty years and still wake up loving one another so can we.*

He had scarred her and then acted as if nothing happened; sorry was the only thing he'd said.

Dana decided at that moment to let it go no matter how she felt. She thought she could put it in the past and make her marriage to Nate work. So, she said a little prayer.

"Lord God help me to truly forgive my husband in my heart. Help me to put the past behind me so that our future is a prosperous one."

Dana prayed that prayer and was done with it.

CHAPTER FIVE

Things were quiet at home as Dana was outback sipping a glass of wine and listening to the radio. It had been nine months since the honeymoon and things were good. Nate was going out every day looking for a job but had not found one yet. They talked and laughed and did things together. Things were looking up for them. Her job kept her very busy. Things had been hectic with the plans to open another restaurant. Nate did not seem to mind when it came to her job. He was supportive of her. Not to mention, it made the days go by faster.

The phone rang, breaking her thoughts. She went into the house to answer it.

"Hello," she answered, but there was silence on the other end, so she hung up. On her way back outside the phone rang again, so she turned around and ran to answer.

"Hello?" This time she heard breathing, so she repeated, "Hello." They hung up on her. She stood there for a moment waiting for it to ring again but it didn't.

Dana decided to lay on the sofa and watch a movie, instead the movie ended up watching her. It was dark when she woke from her nap. She felt more tired now than before her nap. She looked up at the clock. *It's midnight*, she thought, *and Nate still hasn't made it home.* She called his phone, but it went straight to voicemail. She decided to go up to bed. Dana thought about where he could be. She checked her phone to see if he had called her, but he hadn't. She went to bed but not before she called his phone one more time. Again, there was no answer.

The alarm clock went off and Dana growled. She forgot to turn it off. No work today. Although she liked what she did for a living, she liked having a day off better. It gave her time to herself. *Eight o'clock already,* she thought. She tried to roll over for another hour of sleep, but then she heard something coming from outside. She got out of bed to look out of the window.

It was a red truck parked in her driveway with the music blasting.

"You have got to be kidding me!" Dana shouted. "What the hell is she doing here?"

Dana, now irritated, threw on some sweats and a tee shirt then went downstairs to find out what was going on.

She opened the front door and walked up to the truck, it was Nate and the woman she saw at his mother's house.

He rolled down the window. "What's up?" he asked her, in a nonchalant manner. Dana could not believe that's all he had to say to her.

"What's up?" she responded indignantly "It's eight in the morning and you and your friend are blaring music in the driveway."

The woman smirked at her like she had eaten the last cookie out of the cookie jar, Dana looked at her then back at Nate.

"I'll be in, in a minute."

Dana's eyes got bigger when he said that. She looked at the woman sitting in the driver's seat, she was smiling. Dana looked at Nate then back at the broad sitting next to him. "Fine, have it your way," she said as she turned and walked away.

"Bitch who the hell are you talking to?" Nate spat out as he got out of the car.

Dana stopped in her tracks but then decided to keep on walking. When she got into the house, she closed the door and went into the kitchen.

"Bitch!" he yelled. Dana's heart was racing. *How in the hell does he get to stay out all night and then I get called the bitch? What kind of bull is this?*

Nate came in the house and walked to the kitchen where Dana was boiling water. He could see that he had upset her, but it did not matter. "I thought we went through this Dana," he leaned on the wall in the archway of the kitchen.

"Went through what Nate? You not coming home last night or you being with and bringing another woman to our house? If that's what you're talking about, I guess we haven't."

Nate's eyes narrowed as he walked closer to where Dana stood and told her, "I'm talking about the part where I do whatever I damn well please and you have nothing to say about it."

Venom oozed out with every word he said to her. Too close for comfort now, Dana tried to back up, but he caught her arm. "Don't walk away from me when I talk to you," he said through clenched teeth.

She looked at him, eyes wide. She tried to pull away but his grip on her arm tightened. He grabbed her and threw her up against the wall. Dana, angry and scared at the same time, knew what was coming next. *If I'm going to get my ass beat, it won't be for nothing*, she thought. She fought back and stood her ground. Dana ran for the pot of boiling water, but he got to it before her.

Nate was like a panther on the prowl, dragging her from one room to another, bruising her like he did that first time. He kicked and punched her. Dana struggled to get free of him, but the harder she tried the more difficult it was to get away.

"You are a stupid bitch! You think just because you get married, a man is supposed to just be faithful to you? You want the white picket fence with all the trimmings? News flash, men are not faithful to just one woman! Every woman knows that but you! I am supposed to have any woman I want and when I'm ready to come home and be with you then I will. When I'm with you, I'm with you and when I'm not then I'm not!" he spat out at her.

Dana could not believe what she was hearing. Was he serious? Did he truly believe this bull he was talking?

Nate let go of Dana. Her thoughts were going one hundred miles per minute. "Let me explain something to you. You are married to me. I'm married when I want to be!"

Dana sat up on the floor in shock. She fell for his lies and ended up hurt again. *How could I have been so stupid?* Tears were running down her face and her body shook like a leaf. He had managed to make her feel like the smallest insect on earth and she had allowed it. She could not do this anymore.

At that moment, Nate saw every feeling she had for him disappear from her eyes in a matter of seconds. She picked herself up off the floor, walked into the living room, and started to walk up the steps when Nate ran up behind her and rammed her into the wall.

Dana screamed, she felt light headed and it felt as if she would pass out in any moment.

"Stupid bitch!" he called her again then he left out of the house, slamming the door behind him. He made the other woman wait for him while he went in the house to abuse his wife.

Everything she thought was real was a lie. She went upstairs, packed a bag, and left. It seemed as though she drove for hours. She felt numb and exhausted. She ended up going to a hotel in downtown Atlanta; near the underground. There she was close enough to anything she wanted to do.

She put her phone on silent so she could screen her calls. She took her PC with her in case she wanted to do some work. She checked into her room and turned on the TV but could not concentrate on what was playing. Instead, she thought of how the day's events turned out. She thought about the man she called her husband and how he treated her like the biggest joke alive.

Humiliated, depressed and angry, Dana decided that she would no longer give Nate the satisfaction or the power to bring her down.

She went out and got herself something to eat, went to the package store and got herself something to drink to calm her nerves and possibly get some sleep. Then she went back to her room, ate her food, had a couple of drinks and looked at cable until she fell asleep.

Hours passed before she woke up and noticed it had gotten dark outside. Nine o'clock her watch said. She had been sleep for four hours. She flipped through the channels until she found something worth watching. Her thoughts flickered back and forth from the previous night, and the day she got married. Why had not she seen this coming? He had flipped the script so fast she didn't know what hit her besides him. She remembered the woman's face at his mother's house and how she scowled at Dana. *What a joke*, she thought. All the time she was the one who he had been with.

She looked old enough to be his mother. She was a chunky woman, about 5'4" with gold teeth in her mouth. She did not have much of a vocabulary and her mannerisms were of a masculine nature. She also wore a ring on her finger as well. It figures, two cheating ass, disrespecting, stupid people both screwing around on their spouses, neither one of them deserving anything good.

Just then, Dana glanced at her phone. It was blinking, she was getting a call. She picked up her phone saw ten missed messages and another one coming through. Yes, it was Nate and he had been calling her. The phone rang again, and she dropped it as if it burned her. She was determined not to answer for him. He had made his choice and so had she. She lay in the bed stressed to say the least but made up in her mind that she would get the marriage annulled immediately.

She went to sleep with that being the last thing on her mind. Daylight came slowly, maybe because she was exhausted and the fact that she could sleep in peace without having to hold her breath. She slept heavy and it felt like she slept for days. Dana couldn't believe how good she felt. She got out of the bed, brushed her teeth and got to work on her computer looking for lawyers.

She spoke to a couple before making her choice. Two days passed, she took a walk to a nearby restaurant to get something to eat, then she did some window shopping and went back to the room.

She sat in her room switching channels on the TV. She did not know how people could sit home all day every day and do nothing, this would drive her insane. If she could not do something positive, she would go crazy, so she decided that tomorrow she would go back to work.

Her phone had not rung for a couple of hours now and she was sure he was doing something else besides thinking of her. The next morning, she got on the Marta train and headed for work. She thought that if her car was not seen, he would think she was not there in case he was looking for her. If he came in, she would not be visible, she had enough to do in the back anyway.

Dana was going through all the paperwork that was left on her desk. She organized and prioritized what she would do and how she would do it all. She was not there a good hour before she heard loud voices in the front. The door to her office flew open and Nate was there standing in front of her looking like he had not slept in days.

Dana got up quickly, moving backwards but before she could get anywhere, he had leapt across the room screaming at her, "WHERE HAVE YOU BEEN? I've been going out of my mind with worry and why haven't you answered your phone?"

He picked the phone up off the desk and saw that the messages hadn't been looked at, so he hurled the phone across the room breaking it into pieces.

"Why are you here?" Dana tried to ask him in a calm tone, but he ignored her. "Leave this office," she told him. He still ignored her, she reached for the office phone, but he got to it before her. Her heart was beating fast and she tried to think rationally. He grabbed her by the arms and shook her.

"Did you think you could just leave me like that, and I would just let you?"

"Nate, I'm giving you what you want! You want to be with someone else and I want a husband who wants only me. Who wants to love only me and definitely someone who doesn't look at me like I'm their personal punching bag. Why do you think I feel that way Nate? Because I deserve it! I deserve to be happy, not a white picket fence as you call it. If I wanted a picket fence, I'd have one. I've worked too hard for it and I will have it. I want someone who can love me the way I want and need to be loved Nate." She felt faint, realizing she forgot to breathe, but still she continued taking a big breath. "I don't deserve to be treated the way you treat me, and I don't want to be loved the way you love me Nate, it hurts. You hurt Nate. What you say, how you say it and how you do it. So now do what you came to do because this will be the last time you do it!" She looked at him through narrowed eyes, her breathing slightly out of control. Just then, there was a knock at the door.

"Dana," Cliff shouted from the other side "are you alright? Do I need to call the police? Open the door."

"Well Nate," she shrugged, "does he need to call the police?" she asked him with hatred in her eyes.

He looked at her as if he dared her to say yes. She looked at him for one minute before responding, "No, everything is okay. He was about to leave, weren't you Nate?"

He looked at her with contempt but thought better of it, then he turned and walked away. She heard the worker walk away after him.

"I expect to see you within an hour," he spoke as he left out the door.

CHAPTER SIX

Dana, like clockwork walked out the door an hour later. Nate was standing outside in front of his car. "What now Nate she said with hatred dripping from her lips. When she looked at him, he started to say something, but he thought better of it and silence fell between them.

He finally asked her, "Where have you been all this time?"

She sucked in her breath and answered, "I needed time to think," she said.

He watched her as she walked around the car going in the opposite direction of where he was standing.

"I want an annulment," she stated.

He smiled, as he saw her hands tremble slightly, then he looked into her eyes. "Oh! Do you now?" he said in a slow, angry voice. She could hear the poison dripping from his lips. "Here is the thing, when you didn't come home and you didn't answer your phone, I called your son's school to see if you had shown up there. I talked to the school about Eric and told them that we were talking about withdrawing him so that we could be more of a family."

Dana looked on in horror. Eric was her ten-year-old son who went to one of the best schools in

Florida. He was a quiet boy who lived with his grandparents during the school year. He came to spend summer vacation with her. Nate had spent time with them on occasion, the two got along well and that was only because he did not know the Nate she knew, but after the other night Dana had to do whatever it took to keep him away from this monstrosity of a relationship.

"Eric stays in school. He does well there, and I want him in a positive environment," she told Nate.

"Well let's go home and talk about it then."

"Talk about what Nate?" she said in a weary voice. "How I have to sit around and watch as my husband screws anyone he wants to and not have any say in it, or how it gets thrown up in my face? Or are we talking about how I have to get beat over it? Look I know if a person is going to go out and do whatever they want to do that's what they're going to do. No one can stop that person unless they want to. But to do it and make a person deal with it, that's not what I signed up for. I will not live in a prison in my own house. I refuse to do so. You are blatantly disrespecting me, and you are letting her do the same. Can you be tried like that? This female comes to our house Nate, like *so what* and she gets treated like she said I do to you, while I'm treated like the other woman. Who does that?"

Nate heard everything she was saying, he saw the disgust in her face. He heard the hatred in her voice but still repeated to her "Let's go home and talk about it."

"I can't. I have not been here in days and I have

some catching up to do."

"I want you to get in the car right now and come home with me so we can talk about it. Then tomorrow we will plan on going to get Eric from Florida and bring him here to live with us!" he growled.

She looked at him for a brief moment then decided not to protest so she got in the car and agreed to go with him anyway.

On the way home, he took her to get her car and her things from the hotel, then followed her back to the house. Once there, he took her bag to their room. Dana was tired, all she wanted to do was to get away from him. She could not stand being around him anymore, thirteen months was all she could do, and she would do everything she had to do to keep her son away from him.

Just then he came up behind her and put his arms around her. Dana felt so sick she could feel the nausea come up in her mouth and she did what she could to keep it down. She did not want him anywhere around her.

He started kissing her on her neck, feeling her breast and rubbing up against her. The taste of vomit filled her senses as she tried to push it back down. She then pulled away from him. Feeling repulsed, she went and poured herself a drink of cognac straight up to keep herself together. The liquid went down like fire, she winced to keep from gasping because she did not use a chaser. She saw him watching her. He came over to where she was standing, poured her another glass, gave it to her, and she drank it.

His eyes were dark as they peered into hers, she could feel his gaze go straight through her. He took her hand in his and kissed it softly. "You know I love you, don't you?"

Dana looked at him, before she answered, "Love doesn't hurt, hit or betray Nate. You did all three, but who's counting?"

Nate's eyes narrowed when he looked at her, then responded, "Did you honestly think marriage would make me stop having urges for other women Dana?"

"That's what married men do Nate," she responded. "Two shall become as one, that's why they call it marriage."

Feeling agitated, Nate exhaled deeply then finished talking.

"Dana, I have had friends long before I met you, and if I want to have sex with any of them that's what I am going to do. You can't stop a man from being a man and if I come home afterwards and make you suck the scent of them off of me that's what you will do! I want you to remember this; if you ever try and leave again, I will make your son an orphan, and I don't have a problem with that."

Nate turned, walked towards the door, and left. The house was completely silent, the only thing she could hear was her heart beating.

"Father you said that a husband is supposed to love his wives as Christ loves the church. My husband does not, so I ask your forgiveness for

49

being unequally yoked. Free me from this life of abuse before I am only a memory. In Jesus name. Amen."

Alone and feeling more determined than ever. Nate thought he had the upper hand and she would keep on letting him think it. The fact of the matter was when it came to her son, she would do anything she had to do to keep him safe. She would have to plan carefully and tread lightly. Looking at the situation and realizing now, not only was he dangerous, he was also a coward for putting her son in the mix.

Dana poured herself another drink and sat on the couch dumbfounded at how things had turned out after only thirteen months of being married to this man. Never had he shown this side of himself before they were married, but then again, they had only dated a couple of months before she married him. What the hell had she been thinking?

Dana fixed herself another drink and went upstairs to take a bath.

Dana sat in the tub immersed in bubbles with her cognac; trying to make sense out of this mess she had made with her life. She had fallen in love with and married a full-fledged maniac and he showed no signs before then. She laid her head back relaxing in the hot water and lavender scented bubbles, she never thought she would ever be in a situation like this one. Marriage was forever, or so she thought.

She did not know how to feel at this point. Was

she supposed to make her marriage work for the sake of her son's welfare? Was she supposed to turn a blind eye to the mess she created trusting this man and wanting to live with him till they were parted by death? Was she to continue to love him no matter what was happening?

Hell no to all the above, she thought shaking her head. She did not feel loved or respected. She felt as if everything she believed in was a lie, she felt as if she had failed. Dread took over her. She knew she did not want to be in an abusive marriage. Having faith that things would change was one thing, knowing when to get out when they didn't was another.

Dana knew she could not go on being the other woman in her own marriage. She knew that left her no choice but to get out. Nate was not going to let her just walk out and she knew that. She would have to plan everything out, no matter what it took. She would get out of this one way or another.

Feeling a little better from her bath, Dana went downstairs to fix herself something to eat. She really did not have much of an appetite but thought it good to put something on her stomach seeing that she had drank one too many.

The phone rang and she picked it up. "Hello, hey girl is my son there? He promised he would take me grocery shopping and I have been waiting, and what happened to you? He told me you left home and stayed overnight. Now you know that was wrong. I told him you were poison."

"Excuse me?" Dana responded. "I'm poison?

Did he tell you the whole story or just his story?"

"I know one thing, Nate is not going to lie to me, we have a good relationship."

"Okay!" Now this was going too far, she was just as crazy as his ass! "He is not home," Dana responded.

"Home!" she squealed. "You mean he's not there with you," she laughed. "That's okay, I know just where to find him," his mother told her.

Dana could hear the sarcasm in her voice.

"Then why did you call here if you knew where to find him?" Dana was furious now and she hung up the phone before she said something she would regret later. That lady was a piece of work, and if she knew where he was in the first place, she should have called him there, wherever that was.

The rest of the day passed by with ease. No sign of Nate, so all was good, she fell asleep watching TV. She jumped up when she heard the phone ring. She looked up at the wall clock and it was two a.m. The phone rang again; still groggy she looked at it. Who would be calling this time of night? She answered "Hello?"

This time it was the hospital.

"Mrs. Johnson," Dana's eyes widened at the formal way her name was spoken.

"Yes?" she answered.

"This is a nurse from Southern Regional Hospital. I am calling to inform you that your husband was in a car accident and he put you down as his emergency contact."

Dana's heart was thumping hard and fast.

"Is he alright?" she asked.

"Well, yes.   He sustained a couple of head bruises, we need you to come down and sign some papers," the nurse stated.

"Sure of course!   I will be there as soon as I can."

They ended the call.   Dana got out of bed, not really sure how to feel at that moment.   Sure, she still cared for him even after everything that happened, but he had hurt her deeply, physically and emotionally.

My mom was right, you do reap what you sow she said to herself.   She got in the car and headed to the hospital.   She turned on the radio and a familiar tune blared from it, an old Isley Brothers song, so mellow so smooth she hummed along with it.

It was late night, so traffic was not bad like it was during the day.   They stayed near Henry County, so the drive was not long at all.

When she arrived, she saw a familiar face leaving the parking lot.   It was the woman that had been having an affair with her husband.   The woman that had waited in her driveway for her husband while he had come in the house to physically abuse her.   The woman saw her and sped out of the parking lot.   Dana looked at the woman, shook her head and went to take care of the business of the man who would soon be her ex-husband.

When she arrived at the desk the security guard told her which way to go, so she went on to find Nate.   By the time she got to his room he was groggy from the medicine he had received.   The nurse let her know he had asked for her and they told him she was on the way.

I bet you did, Dana thought to herself as she remembered the female leaving the parking lot like a bat out of hell. The nurse filled her in on what was going on and what the doctor's orders were.

He called for her when he heard them whispering. She answered him and walked around the bed to face him. He looked at her, his eyes watering and he apologized to her for the other night. That stunned her! She did not think he was coherent enough to remember anything right now. She was not expecting that at all.

He held out his hand for her and she hesitated for a moment before she took it. "I promise you that I will never hurt you again, I know what I did was wrong, and I love you."

Dana looked down at Nate laying in the hospital bed looking very vulnerable. He was almost believable had she not almost got run over by the bat out of hell out in the parking lot.

CHAPTER SEVEN

Dana's eyes widened as Nate continuously apologized to her again and again, only this time he promised that they could go and talk to someone, anything she wanted he would do. He was admitting he was wrong and telling her he was willing to seek help for their marriage in the same breath. *Boy they must have given him some good shit,* she thought.

She paused for a long time, just looking at him in his eyes.

"Please give me another chance, and say you love me too," he pleaded.

Dana did not notice the tears coming from her eyes when she looked down at his face. The only thing she could say to him was, "Yes I do love you, but it's not enough if there isn't going to be any respect and change involved."

He shook his head and nodded off to sleep.

Her eyes closed because she knew she still had feelings for him and she married him, but now there was something else. Dana knew she couldn't sell her soul to the devil for the sake of love or marriage. She feared that since she'd admitted to him that she still had feelings for him, it would give him more ammunition to treat her bad. Did she truly believe things would change between she and Nate? Did she want them to? She watched him in this groggy state and her answer was no.

Nate was released from the hospital today. He'd been there for two days because the doctor wanted to make sure all the test came back good before they let him come home. He seemed to be in good spirits, so things were more friendly than usual. Dana went with the flow and enjoyed the ride until she could do something else. Dana did not mention anything about seeing the woman in the red truck the night she got the call to come to the hospital. She felt that if she agreed to give him another chance, she should be the wife he wanted her to be, so that's what she was going to do for now.

When they arrived home, she helped him up the stairs and went to run a shower for him. He was still having headaches, but the doctor assured them they would go away soon.

Once in the bedroom, she put his things away and started to go into the bathroom. Before she got to the archway, he called out to her. "Dana," he said softly.

She turned around as he walked up to her and before she could say anything, he kissed her so long and soft that it took her a minute to get her thoughts together. She tried to push him away, but he wouldn't let her. His hands went around her body and he cupped her buttocks, then they traveled up her body. Slowly he pulled back and took her by the hand, leading her to the bed. She tried to protest because the doctor said he had to rest and not to do anything strenuous.

He kissed her again and Dana allowed him to, her breath was a little more ragged now as he started undressing, kissing and licking her in every place he removed clothing from. She stood in front of him naked and trembling, he looked at her for a moment then he laid her on the bed.

Dana's eyes widened with nervousness and passion as she saw the intensity in his face. She waited for him to take his clothes off, but he never did. He parted her legs and kissed and teased each one of her thighs ever so slowly, licking and nibbling until he felt her shiver in anticipation. Dana trembled at the feel of his lips and his tongue as he got closer to the center of her most delicate piece of flesh. She hissed and sighed at the softness of his tongue teasing her, this sent her senses into overdrive. She could barely breath and felt her body go weak as he licked and sucked on her in a slow, gentle and steady rhythm; sending her to a place that she could only imagine.

Dana's mind was shattering like glass as she was taken beyond the point of no return and the beat of her heart grew faster. No one had ever given her such pleasure orally. She put her hands around his head as he gave her mind-blowing head, she moaned again, that was the only thing she could do to keep herself from passing out. When she felt her body stiffen, jerk, and tremble Dana released one orgasm and then another until she lost count. Tears streamed down her face as her body twitched and jerked then went limp. She lay there for what seemed like an eternity until she could get her mind back intact.

Nate laid beside her, rubbing her breasts, her stomach, and her neck as he watched her come back from that place she had journeyed to in her time of ecstasy. When she opened her eyes, he was looking down at her smiling. She almost forgot how he looked when he smiled at her, and it did something to her, made her feel like he truly loved her.

Shaking her head and coming back to her senses she reminded herself, *it was only head girl get your mind right.* No one ever went down on her and made her feel like that before. The way he pleasured her made him a candidate in the vote for head president, and he'd win hands down.

He studied her for a long time; her eyes, her lips, the way she watched him. Then he smirked and said, "If I did ever let you leave, *and I'm not*, you will not be able to be with another man ever. You would not be right for any other man and they would not be able to get close to you in anyway shape or form."

Dana narrowed her eyes at him, what he said shook her out of the luxurious state she was in. She responded back, "Only a man like you could make a woman feel the way you just made me feel and only the devil can take it away."

He looked at her and smiled. "So, which one do you think I am?"

Things were alright with them it had been two months since the accident and life was low key.

Dana was the only one working, Nate had lost his job the day the first incident happened. So,

Dana took care of everything. Nate would go out every morning looking for work, so she believed, but by time he got home it was usually bedtime. Dana was not blind to the fact that he was seeing someone else and she had a guess as to who that someone was, so she went about her days working and taking care of home.

One day, they went to his mother's house. She had broken her hip going down some stairs, so they went over to help her with some things. *That's what happens when you're evil*, Dana thought while she went grocery shopping for her, cleaned her house and all the while she talked shit. The kicker was that when she took her medication, she started talking non-stop.

Nate went on an errand for her and while he was gone, she started telling me how they didn't make women like me anymore. "You are from the decade of the 50s."

Bitch, Dana thought as she listened to the ghetto banshee. His mother laughed as she told Dana that no matter what she did, she would never have Nate the way she wanted him. She then went on to say that she made him promise her that he would never love any woman more than her. She taught him how to dog and control women, never to trust or love them and always have an ace in the hole because no one woman would love him for him.

She listened in amazement as this basket case told her these things.

Mildred told her that if she wanted to keep her marriage, she had a person she could call and all she'd need was some underwear. She showed her a book of chants and tried to get her to read it. Dana listened to her and thought the woman was a real lunatic. Dana looked at her mother-in-law and started rebuking her and all of her spirits.

People don't understand why they go through what they go through, why their life is so bad. It's because of people like her, Dana thought.

She got her purse off of the dining room table along with her keys and left. Dana wondered how Nate got around, and she called him to let him know she was going home. She had had enough of Broom Hilda and all of this madness, Dana didn't want to be around it or Mildred a second more. Dana laughed as she dialed her husband's number. She had heard it all. What kind of woman would teach a kid the things her mother-in-law taught her own son? She shook her head as she waited for him to answer the phone.

"Hello," he answered.

"Hi, are you far away?"

"Yes," he answered.

"Well I am not feeling well, and I am on the way home," Dana told him still thinking about his mother.

"Okay I'll be alright. Go ahead, I'll get a way," he answered her.

"Alright then, I will see you later."

Dana pulled up in the driveway glad to be home. She noticed a faint smell when she opened the door. *What is that?* She thought to herself. She tried to follow the smell through the house but could not find where it came from, so she opened every window in the house to air it out.

It was a beautiful day out and all the flowers were in bloom. The different mixture of smells lit up the downstairs area as the wind blew through the windows.

It puzzled her as to where the smell came from but since she did not find anything, she chalked it up to the house being closed up. She opened up the patio doors and thought it would be nice to sit on the deck with a glass of wine. The more she thought of what her mother-in-law told her, the more she felt as if she was in a bad b rated movie. *And the hits just keep on coming,* she thought.

She was a newlywed of eighteen months, with a cheating husband and a mother-in-law who needed to be in the psych ward on the thirteenth floor. They say crack kills. Dana shook her head as she murmured to herself in prayer;

"Father God, thank you for surrounding me with your protection. Thank you for guiding me in how I deal with people and for helping me to treat them with love no matter how they treat me or what they say to me. I ask you to bless the ones who try and hurt me in any way. Thank you for putting my enemies under Your feet. In Jesus name, Amen."

CHAPTER EIGHT

Dana noticed the sun going down, but took her time about going inside. It was a beautiful day and one thing was for sure, there is no place like home. She glanced at her watch, it was nine o'clock, and she had not heard from Nate. She decided to call him, but when she dialed the number he did not pick up.

It was eleven o'clock when Nate decided to come home. When he walked in the door, he appeared to be upset about something. It was not long before Dana realized what was going on. It took a couple of slammed doors, a broken glass and a few sarcastic words before she realized that he wanted a reason to leave again. She looked at him and asked him if he needed anything before, she went upstairs to bed. He had a frustrated look on his face that told her he was ready to pounce, so she bid him goodnight and left.

Nate paced downstairs where Dana left him, his head whirling with the images of having sex with the other woman, the things she whispered in his ears, the thoughts she left burning in his mind. He shook his head laughing to himself. He had been involved with this woman for four years, she was married and that's the only reason he married Dana. Dana was different. She was a quiet gentle woman.

He could trust her to be faithful, to do anything it took to make him happy and she had a way about her that made anybody who met her like her instantly. She was what a lot of people would call a good girl. *So why am I with her*, he asked himself. He shook his head as he thought of an answer, then he smiled at his reply.

When he laid his head down at night, he did not have to worry about hot burning sugar or grits being thrown on him for the dirty shit he did to women. Nevertheless, they were married now, and he would kill her before he let anyone else have her. The thought of that stirred something in him because he saw the change in her and how she looked at him these days. In just so little time he had taken the sweetest of smiles and turned it into disgust. This made Nate a little heated so he would go do what he did best.

Dana was in the bed when Nate entered the room. Her eyes were closed, but she heard and felt him as he walked across the room. The hair stood up in the back of her neck as she heard him breathing. Just then he called her name. Her eyes opened as she answered him.

"Yes."

He looked at her with the appearance of a snake, his eyes small as he slithered across to her. "I'll be back sometime tomorrow," he said.

She looked at him and answered, "Okay Nate," before she closed her eyes again.

All of a sudden, she was jumping up holding her face. "WHY DID YOU SLAP ME?" she yelled.

He pounced on her so quickly it almost knocked the breath out of her and before she knew it, he was choking her.

"So now you don't care?" he said as he tightened his grasp around her neck. Dana was now trying to break free from his grip and all she heard coming from him was, "You don't care bitch? You don't care if I go?"

Now free, Dana jumped off the bed and tried to make it to the cell phone on the dresser, but he beat her to it, snatched it off the dresser and threw it out of the room. She could hear it shatter into pieces. Stunned she looked at him in dismay holding her face.

"What the hell is wrong with you and why did you hit me? You said you were leaving, I said okay."

He jumped to where she stood and slapped her again. This time she flew over the bed and hit her head on the edge of the dresser. Feeling light headed, she fell into a deep sleep. When Dana woke up, she felt sluggish, her head hurt, and she was a bit foggy on what happened. She was still on the floor, then she remembered last night. Nate, the slap, the phone. She got up and sat on the edge of the bed trying to get herself together. Her head was throbbing. After a couple of minutes, she walked over to the bedroom window, looked out, and saw the car gone. He left, after doing what he did, he left. He didn't check on her, but left her for dead, lying on the floor. Dana sighed a breath of relief that she was okay and that she was alone. She was ready to make her move. She went downstairs and noticed the telephone cord yanked out of the wall. Wow! He destroyed the telephone cord.

She shook her head and went into the kitchen to make a cup of coffee. She sat at the table, her thoughts scattering all over the place. Her first thought was Eric, she had to make other arrangements for him, and she had to keep him safe. She had to put all of her ducks in a row if this was going to work. She thought and thought. She carefully planned everything she had to do, how and when it had to happen. She broke out into laughter, you would have thought she was trying to get away from the mafia or something. This was one man and if she knew the right man, she could have his ass beat!

There goes that smell again, she winced.

It was stronger today than it was the day before. *Where was it coming from?* She got up and started sniffing around trying to follow the smell. The closer she got to the kitchen sink the worse the smell became. She started for the cabinets opening each one. When she came to the middle cabinet, she gasped! It smelled like something was dead. There under the sink was a bag. She took it from underneath and opened it up. She shrieked back in horror. There was a soiled maxi pad and a dead bird in the bag. She coughed and gagged, her stomach going into a frenzy of spasms, she jumped up and ran to the back door and immediately got rid of the bag. She ran back in the house and opened all the windows from the kitchen to the living room spraying Lysol and pouring bleach underneath the sink trying to get rid of that awful smell. Her thoughts went back to his mother and the conversation they had only days ago. Her thoughts were going from Nate to his crazy, deranged ass mom. What the hell was he trying to do? She felt the nausea swelling up in her throat as she remembered that terrible smell. She went upstairs to take a shower, the smell from under the sink was stuck in her head and throat. She let the hot water run all over her calming her senses as she thought over the situation, her head was still aching. You had to be mad, even demonic to do something as nasty and trifling as that.

After the shower, she anointed her head with blessing oil and went into the closet. Dana prayed constantly. It was the only thing that kept her sane. She prayed hard, she prayed faithfully and all the time. When she finished, she heard a noise. When she turned her head, she could see Nate peeking in the cracked door at her, this made her shiver a little. She got up, threw on some jeans and a t shirt took the oil while he was looking and went downstairs to anoint under the sink where the devil had tried to take her out.

He followed her, watching her every move, eyeing her like a hawk and when she turned his way, she saw the strangest smile on his face. His eyes were narrowed almost into a slit, she looked at him without breaking down. *The devil himself,* she thought.

"Guess what I found underneath the sink

today?" He said nothing but still watched her, as she continued, "I found a dead bird and a bloody pad. Hmm, wonder how that got there," she finished.

He sneered at her and replied, "You think you have all the sense, don't you? Be glad it was not anything else," he stated.

Dana swung around swiftly. "Why did you marry me?" she asked.

"Because I'm grown and you?" he asked.

"I thought I loved you," was her reply. She turned to leave the kitchen and go to the living room when a knife flew by her and hit the wall, sticking straight through it.

"The next time I won't miss."

Her heart started beating faster, but she acted as if she did not see it.

"I am going to the store to get dinner," she said knowing all along that when she left, she was going straight to the police station.

"No, I'm going with you," was his reply.

She sighed, "Fine."

At the grocery store she tried to stall as long as she could, picking up items she knew she did not need or want. She just needed to get out of the house to think about things other than the spawned demon child himself. She even gave him a new name. She had not looked at him the same since that first night he had put his hands on her. Although she had forgiven him for it then, the fact that he did it again brought that all back. Now she had to plan to get away, not walk out her door like normal people. She had to literally plan her get away to be safe. But you had better believe this was not going to be in vain.

Back in the car and heading home the air was thick and neither said anything to the other. *Home,* she thought. She used to think of this as home, but now it was just a lavish prison. Looking at the front door as they pulled up, she got out and walked to the door and opened it. I *miss work,* she thought.

She had not been back since the day he came home from the hospital. The owners were really nice about it. They told her to take as much time as needed with pay as long as she came back ready to work. But she would not be back anytime soon. Not until her life was stable again. Dana's whole demeanor started changing and she started to withdraw. She did not say too much unless she had too. Life had gone from bad to worse and all she longed for was an ending to it all. Not only did she need peace of mind, she wanted it and was determined to somehow get it.

"I'm going to take a shower," was all he told her while watching her walk into the kitchen to cook something to eat. Dana did not bother to turn around to face or acknowledge him, she just continued walking.

She really did not have an appetite for one, but she threw some steaks on the grill anyway. She was pouring herself a glass of wine when she heard a car horn beeping in her driveway. She walked to her door and opened it. The woman with the red truck yelled out of the window, "Tell Nate I'm here."

Dana was furious. *This chick has some nerve*, she thought. "Tell Nate I'm here? Who..." before she could finish what she was saying, she was being pulled into the house, the door slamming.

"Look, when someone comes here for me you don't ask any questions," Nate fumed.

Dana was fuming now too. "What do you mean? First of all, she bumped her horn, secondly 'tell Nate I'm here,'" she mocked the woman's voice, "who the hell does she think she is? You don't come to someone's house and tell a man's wife to tell him she's here. That was disrespectful and you are disrespectful for letting it happen. What if that was another man-," before she could finished that last statement, he grabbed her hair and punched her to the floor.

"First of all, that would not be another man, secondly my friends are always welcome to come over my house whenever I want them to, and you don't have any say so when it comes to my friends at all. The ones before you and the ones I meet in the future."

"To hell with you Nate! Why don't you get out of my life?" she asked him. His eyes widened as he pounced on top of her and started banging her head to the floor. The horn bumped again, and he stopped. He got up and left out of the door.

Dana got off the floor crying. Now fed up, angry and sick and tired of being sick and tired, Dana went to the neighbor's house and asked to use the phone; it was there she called the police. When they got there, they asked the usual questions, surveyed her face and told her, "Ma'am there is nothing we can do seeing there are no visible bruises to your face or body and no witnesses to the actual confrontation. Our hands are tied when it comes to domestic situations and unless there is any damage and or danger of any kind, we cannot step in."

Dana looked at the officer in astonishment. "You mean to tell me my husband can abuse me all he wants and if there are no bruises, I can't get any help from you? That's a bunch of bull! What about protect and serve? What if it's too late?"

"I'm sorry ma'am," was all the officer could say.

Dana was blown away to say the least. They left and she sat in the living room still in disbelief on what the police had told her. When you couldn't even call the police for help you were up the creek without a paddle. You have some innocent men who get arrested and or killed for doing nothing. Some have been falsely accused, some even get the death penalty. A man hits his wife and they can't do anything without seeing a bruise? Feeling beyond angry, Dana thought *what do I have to do? Die before action is taken?*

Dana felt all alone with no one to talk to and no one to ask for help. She closed her eyes and prayed;

"Lord God please give me peace that surpasses all understanding and the strength to get through it all."

CHAPTER NINE

What was it about this female that makes me not care about anything else? Nate thought. *Hell, she was here before Dana and for another reason she been down since I met her, she's married yes but she makes sure I come first. You would think I was married to her the way I'm always with her. More than my own wife.*

His thoughts were all tangled up into this woman he laid on top of at this moment, trying to beat a hole through her back. She moaned as he stroked harder and harder. Shit, this wasn't the best piece of ass he had ever had, but this is what he was used to, banging it out whenever he wanted. She moaned again as she squeezed his ass, "Oh baby, yes. Tell me I'm better than your wife," she said to him. The more she talked, the more she moaned, the harder he pumped in her and she loved every minute of it. He never had to say a word. The fact was that no, she wasn't better than Dana, but then again Dana wasn't like other women either. They just didn't make women like her anymore. *I guess the more hood a broad is the more it turns me on*, Nate thought. *Dana isn't that woman.* She was too much of a goodie-goodie, not dirty enough, but this one right here, she was down with whatever. *I could make this chick rob a bank and she would take the rap just so I wouldn't go to jail. Plus, she gives me whatever I want, hell she would sell her house just to make sure I stayed with her. Anyway, it's just the thrill of the game that I like,* he thought. *Hell, why not have my cake and eat it too? Whose going to stop me?*

He thought of Dana, then he looked down at the other woman while he stroked her long and hard and said to himself *hell, she isn't going anywhere. Mom dukes saw to that with her gifts,* he smiled and at that thought, he released and gave all he had to give for that moment to the other woman.

Later he lay beside the sleeping woman, wondering what the hell was he doing and why? He could remember talks he had with his mother long ago, her telling him how to control women.

"You make them love you hard, then you leave them without a warning. This confuses them because they don't understand how, why and what hit them and when you go back to them, they will do anything you want," she told him.

He remembered his mother making him promise that he wouldn't love any woman more than he loved her. She told him that he could always use her house to bring his other women over and screw them if he needed and to just make sure he got their money when they were through.

He remembered taking underwear home to his mother, the ones he wanted to keep around they stayed. The ones he didn't left as quickly as they came. Dana though she never liked, but told me to keep her around because she helped her out with money and anything else she needed. The reason I managed to keep everything as quiet as I did before we got married was because Dana always worked long hours and she traveled a lot for her job. It was easy to make time for her, it was easy to be with her without any mishaps.

She loved me once, I know this just by the look in her eyes and even though she is going through things, that love she felt for me was real and it gave me the upper hand and that's why she's never going to leave. My mother always told me that women who love hard will work through anything. The worse you treat a woman the more love and loyalty they have for you. He looked over at the other woman lying beside him. He did have feelings for her. Hell, she paid mom's rent and gave her a healthy allowance every month. He should have said something to her about coming to the house whenever she wanted earlier but decided against it. She didn't come for Dana, she came for me. *If Dana can't accept my past, then she will not be accepted as my future. I made my side piece feel like she is more important than my wife by giving her that status and I made my wife a side piece because I can. This is who I am and I'm not going to stop being me for no one, and if she tries to leave again, well, we would just take a trip to the Chattahoochee river.*

Just then the other woman turned over, saw him awake and started stroking his flesh to hardness. *Round two,* he thought.

Being with this woman was better than being home laying with his wife. He knew he wouldn't

73

give her what she really deserved. He was better off where he was at and that was with a woman who had no respect for her husband, her marriage or herself. *Two peas in a pod me and her*, he thought as he rolled on top of her.

He would keep her loving him just because she did, and he'd make her respect him while doing it. *What am I getting from it?* he thought intently. A trophy when he wanted one. An obedient one at that. She gave him something he had never had in his life and that was a woman who cared and respected the laws of life. He never knew what that meant until he met her. She taught him more than what his mother ever did. To be honest, everything he wanted in a mother, she was it, only now he got the best of both worlds.

"I love you Nate," the other woman whispered in his ears while he pumped her slowly and deeply sending trimmers through her body one after another with every stroke. He didn't reply but kept up the rhythm by going deeper and deeper until she cried out his name.

He made love to her with such passion that she released with a series of tears and then fell back to sleep in his arms from the exhaustion of tonight's sex session.

Nate looked down at her and smiled. *My mission is complete. One satisfied woman tonight and a new car for mom in the morning.* Nate knew he could be arrogant at times, but he didn't care. Women had it their way for years, so he wasn't going to feel bad about doing what he did and that's get what he wants when he wants it.

Dana lay in her bed tears streaming down her face, enough was enough and she was sick and tired of being sick and tired.

How could this man that she thought she loved, turn a switch on her so fast that she felt like a complete fool?

She had married a man that didn't give a damn about her, her feelings or the fact that they were married and now he wouldn't let her just walk out of this marriage.

She sobbed deeply for her heart was truly heavy. She had held it in pretty much since that first night. She was angry and disappointed, not only with him, but with herself as well. This man came into her life and married her just to treat her like she was nothing and she had let him. She cried all night until she cried herself to sleep. Her dreams were of happier times when Nate loved her, and he didn't mind showing her. Dana in return loved him and when they made love, he would touch her body with sensual caresses and loving kisses and teasing, sending her body through waves of sexual intensity.

She dreamed of how he would hold her when it was over kissing her all over her body and rubbing her body as if he was starting the fire all over again.

Dana slept peacefully for the rest of the night, not budging from the spot in which she laid. In fact, she slept so good that when she woke up it was ten am. She laid there not in any hurry to get up. She didn't know what she would face today, but whatever it was, she had to prepare for it.

Depression started to take her without warning, and she knew she had to hold on for the sake of herself. She couldn't let him see her sweat no matter what he did or said to her.

She struggled to get out of bed and the longer she laid there the harder it became to get out.

"Okay, girl, get it together," she said as she put one foot on the floor then the other one. She looked at herself in the mirror. Her eyes were different, they had bags under them from crying herself to sleep and lines in the corner from worry. She put on her eyeliner and a pair of form fitting jeans, a shirt that fit her just as nicely as the jeans and then put the finishing touches of her makeup on, making sure her lip gloss popped when she smiled. Her breast looks perkier than she remembered. She took her hair down and let it cascade all around her shoulders and down her back. She stepped back in the mirror and stared appreciatively at herself.

"This is the day that the Lord has made I will rejoice and be glad in it."

Dana spoke these words of encouragement over herself and then she left the room to get her day started. Once downstairs, she opened the curtains and the blinds letting all the sunshine in, then she went to the kitchen, made herself a cup of coffee, sat down and mapped out her day. School would be out in four months. She would start from there, she would make arrangements for Eric, so he did not have to be here when everything finally went down.

Dana took her car keys off of the table in the living room and left the house. Today she had to replace the phone Nate broke the other night. She would then make the necessary calls to ensure her son's safety, and placement for his vacation. She would also go to the market and shop like she was celebrating. She would buy a couple of steaks and some crabs to go on the grill and may even invite guests over.

Dana got into her car, started it up and turned on her radio then headed down the road bobbing her head from side to side to the music that was playing. She had planned the day as if she was happily single, taking care of the most important business first. Her get away. It's been two whole years since she and Nate got married and after she was free from this ordeal, she promised herself that she would not give her heart to anyone else. No man would ever break through what was once freely given. She had paid the price one time and there would not be another, because she did not have it in her heart to trust anyone else. Her heart belonged only to her son now. He needed her, and she would be there to raise him to be the man he was supposed to be. She would teach him to never use, misuse and abuse women ever. How could somebody actually make a person believe that they are something totally different than what they were?

Stopping at a red light, Dana did not notice the red truck two cars behind her. When the light turned green, she preceded down the street. Nate noticed her instantly and wondered where she was going, so he decided to follow her. The woman sitting beside him noticed and grew agitated when she saw what he was doing.

"I thought we were going to eat," she told him. "Why are you following her wh..." but before she could finish her statement Nate shot her an angry look of frustration. The other woman's mouth snapped shut and she looked out of the passenger side window.

Dana's, first stop was to get a new phone, so she drove up in the parking lot of metro pcs, parked the car and got out. She still did not notice the red truck or her husband with the other woman. Nate smiled as she walked into the store and the other woman eyed her taking in every curve of Dana's body and every sway of the rhythm in her walk with hatred.

She may be married to him, but he sleeps in my bed, the other woman smiled as she thought to herself. She looked over at Nate like the cat that ate the canary. He looked back at her and rolled his eyes.

CHAPTER TEN

It took all of twenty minutes to get a new phone and when Dana stepped out of the store with her new phone in her hand a few men walking by her tried to talk to her, but she just kept on walking not even acknowledging them. Back in the car now and off to the grocery store to get something to eat, Dana thought about a menu as she passed the traffic lights. She dialed her job to check in. Dwayne answered the phone.

"Thank you for calling Charlie D's where your dining experience is a good one."

"Hi Dwayne, this is Dana."

"Dana! What a surprise, how are you?"

Dana giggled at the sound of his voice. "Good how are things there? I miss you all so much."

Dwayne replied, "We miss you too."

"When are you coming back to work? You know this place needs your expertise and that wonderful smile of yours."

"Well I hope to be back soon."

"My darling and how is life going back at the dungeon? You know, the sooner you get away from that trifling, no good monster of yours the better off you'll be."

Dana giggled but she knew he was right; Nate was not the most discrete person when it came to what was going on lately. He had managed to get himself banned from the restaurant after the little fiasco he caused in the first year of their marriage.

Dana replied, "Well Dwayne keep your fingers crossed and hope for the best."

"Hmmm! Do I smell a plan sweetie?" Dwayne asked.

Dana giggled again and answered "How inquisitive of you Sir, but I can't go into anything right now. Look what are you doing later? I am throwing some steaks on the grill along with some crab legs and popping a bottle of wine," Dana told him.

"Oh! That sounds great but tonight I have a hot date. I'll be popping a few bottles myself if I'm lucky," Dwayne said.

"Who is the lucky suitor this time?" Dana asked him.

"You don't know him," Dwayne answered. "I just met him and let me tell you he is one hot ass number."

"Sounds like a sure thing," Dana giggled.

"But of course, you have to be to deal with me," Dwayne laughed "But let's do a rain check."

"Sounds good! Have a great time and don't do anything I would not do," Dana said.

"Don't worry sweetheart I am going to do everything you don't do, now get out of my pocket I have work to do."

"Ok," Dana answered. "Talk to you soon, bye."

Dana finished all of her shopping without a glimpse of the red truck that was following her.

"If I would have known we were playing I spy today following your wife around I would have stayed home," the woman said in an angry tone.

"If I want to follow my wife all day long then that's what I'll do whether you're along for the ride or not. As a matter of fact, I'll do what I damn well please whenever I feel like it, and you'll deal with it as usual."

The angry woman huffed but not before she answered, "Understood." Then she tried to lighten the conversation up by pouting her lips and changing her tone to a more sensual and light hearted one. "Baby you promised we were going to have a special day just you and me."

Nate looked at her with frustration in his eyes but softened up just a bit. He looked up to see if he could see Dana driving up ahead when he saw her turning the corner.

Nate cursed to himself, looked at the woman sitting next to him and rolled his eyes. Then off the other way they went.

Dana was feeling good about herself for the first time in a long time as she drove up to her house to enjoy the rest of her day. Back in the house, Dana put on her favorite Isley Brothers CD, poured herself a glass of wine and went to start the grill. It was a beautiful day. March was one of her favorite months because the flowers were blooming, and the grass smelled wonderful, especially when it was freshly cut.

It was not cold, and it was not hot, but just right for this time of year. The Isley Brothers CD was blaring through the house with their sultry sound of the seventies that made her feel relaxed and gave her a certain peaceful demeanor. Back in the kitchen she cut up lettuce, tomatoes, and cucumbers for a salad, and put a couple of potatoes in the oven. She put a pot of water on to steam her crab legs her mouth watered at the meal she would be eating today. She sat outside and waited for the coals on the grill to die down so she could slow cook her freshly marinated steaks. She thought about the days to come, and what she needed to do to prepare for the days ahead. Her future.

"Father I praise you for today and every day in my life. I thank you for your protection and I ask you for guidance in my journey. Help me to do what's right for me and my child. Take me away from this mess and set me back on track. In Jesus name."

She would go somewhere she and her son could live in peace. She had saved some money up in a separate account just in case of a rainy day.

Dana had always had two accounts, one to live on and one for emergencies. Especially with Nate stealing money out of her purse every chance he got. She had to keep a secret account.

Her mother had taught her that long ago, you have incidentals and must haves, that means an allowance for what you need and an allowance for what you want.

It was the same here, an account for what you

need and an account for dire straits, meaning life or death.

The day turned into evening, the evening turned into night and all was good because Dana had peace of mind being alone and by herself. Dana had always prided herself on treating others as she wanted to be treated. The only thing with that was she did not always get treated the way she treated people. Some people thought she was soft because she refused to befriend people for what she could get from them. Why smile in someone's face when you're really not feeling it? She'd rather not deal with people if she had to pretend to feel a certain way when she did not. People want what they're not willing to give and the more you give a person the more they feel their entitled to, or they think you owe them. Dana meditated on that thought alone and when she finished, she said to herself; *well as of right now, I have paid my dues, I am debt free and I owe it to myself to remove those from my life who take and do not give. Your reign is over!* Dana thought of Nate, *how do you demand respect when you don't give it?*

Dana suddenly understood why women who are complete bitches treat men the way they do, why men who are complete womanizers who don't give a damn about women treat them the way they do. That's because somewhere down the line they have been shitted on by the other sex in some way. She didn't agree with their methods, but she did understand. The bottom line is, you do get back what you give, somewhere down the line. Some people put themselves in positions to be treated a certain way, even though it's not right, and when that person comes along who is right for you, the ones who deserve a good and committed person loses out. But then again, you have people who only love people who treat them like shit. A match made in heaven or a glutton for punishment.

I know I deserve happiness and someone good because I've never treated anyone like shit. I have loved deeply, surely and hard. I have given all I have and all that I am, but there comes a time in your life when enough is enough.

All of this went through Dana's mind as she sat on the patio sipping her wine. *It's time to fight back, I am not a victim and I refuse to be one.* Dana's thoughts were raging to say the least and she went through details in her mind. How could she let this man have a hold on her the way he did? She was going to get herself together, and Nate could do whatever the hell he wanted to do without her. Dana immediately called the owners of the restaurant and made arrangements to go back to work. She had always had her own, never depending on anyone and that's how she would keep it. If Nate wanted to live his life like an unmarried man, then she would let him do it. She had plans of getting the hell out of this situation and he was not going to stop her!

She knew he would never let her walk out that easily, so she had to do it in a way that did not cause drama. One way or the other she was leaving, and she would never look his way again. She took another sip of wine. She never saw this coming, she would not have thought in a thousand years, this was going to be her life. She made the mistake of a lifetime but wouldn't make it twice.

Taking another sip of wine, she kept thinking that it was just a matter of time.

"You never miss your water until your well runs dry. That's the way I was taught, and grandma was never wrong."

"Father thank you for opening my eyes. I realize that I've been unequally yoked for some time now, and I ask that you free me from this bondage. I promise that I will never put myself in this position ever again In Jesus name."

CHAPTER ELEVEN

Tonight, was a good night, Dana thought as she washed her body in the shower. These couple of days alone were as peaceful as could be and she was beginning to like the feel of that. No Nate, no arguing, no bruises, just pure, blissful peace. He did not know that she spotted him following her today while he was with the other woman. She smiled to herself, nodding her head as she remembered earlier that day acting like she didn't see him. She wanted to seem as smooth as silk and she wanted him to see her that way. The nerve of him. He had not been home in days and he's following her. *This man is a real piece of work.*

Later on, while lying in bed, Dana thought of the days to come. She would be back at work and on her way to becoming a free woman again. She would find another place to live and start her life over. She knew that after this she would swear off relationships. She learned that love doesn't love anyone which taught her that there was no such thing as love in human form. It just did not exist, not when it came to her anyway.

She fell asleep with a bit of hope, making her feel a little more confident in how things would turn out. She slept peacefully never feeling the presence of the man standing over her looking down at her.

It was five o'clock in the morning when she moved in her sleep. She could hear breathing coming from someone other than herself. She opened her eyes in alarm to see Nate sitting in a chair next to her side of the bed. He looked to be in deep thought never taking his eyes off of her. She laid there not saying anything not knowing what type of mood he was in. He just sat there looking at her as if he was dissecting every inch of her. She got out of bed and went into the bathroom. She closed the door and stood for a moment trying to calm her breathing. How long had he been there? How long had he been looking at her and what was he thinking about doing this time?

She had finished using the bathroom and was washing her hands. She looked in the mirror at her reflection. Just the sight of him and the very presence of him wrecked the calmness and serenity she felt. She needed peace of mind and she was going to get it. When she walked out of the bedroom, he was still sitting in the chair she had left him in. She walked over to the bed and laid back down like him being there did not bother her. It was quiet for a while, and then Nate spoke.

"Do you think I'm stupid Dana?"

She looked at him trying not to let fear or anger take her over.

She had not seen him in days and the first thing he wanted to do when he did see her was argue. She would not give him the satisfaction.

"Nate, what are you talking about?" she asked him trying to keep her voice intact. "It's five in the morning and I have no idea what you are referring to."

"You think I don't know about your other man?" he scowled at her.

Her eyes widened in disbelief as she repeated "ANOTHER MAN!"

"Who the hell is he?" Nate asked in a voice that dripped of wrath.

Anger taking her now, but remaining calm she responded, "Nate, first of all I don't have another anything! You must have mistaken me with you. Secondly, I am not the one running around town with someone else, that's you! Thirdly you haven't been home in days and the first thing you want to do when you do come home is accuse me of another man at five o'clock in the morning? You have shown me that I can't trust a man any more than I can throw one. I don't accuse you of what I see with my own eyes, so don't accuse me of what you don't see. I'm the one who is a prisoner in is this house Nate, not you. I'm the one who goes to bed at night alone Nate, not you. And I'm the one who is in bed by myself when you're not here Nate, not you. Besides, you do what you want to do right? Isn't that what you said? I have come to grips with that. You like it, I love it. So, let's drop this thing you call an argument, because I refuse to be lured into one. I'm doing everything you want me to do whether I like it or not." Her body shook with anger and Nate could see it. His eyes narrowed as he looked at Dana.

She turned to walk out of the room then Nate

stopped her in her tracks. "Just remember what I said Dana, I don't mind getting rid of my problems babe."

Dana turned her head slightly around not looking all the way back. She responded; "Nate a problem always has a solution, if you can't fix a problem then it's not a problem unless you make it one." She walked out of the room and went down the stairs.

He stood in the room by himself taking in her shape. The gown she wore was so thin that he could see every curve of her body. She had a body that curved in all the right places and every time he looked at her, he would get an erection. She had a pretty face and she always smelled so damn good. She was a lot prettier than what he was used to dealing with. He could remember when they were dating how men would look at her. She carried herself with class always. When he asked her to marry him, he did not think she would say yes, and when she did the quest for her died out.

He went through with the ceremony because he felt like he would always have something to fall back on with her.

He shook his head to himself, he knew he was a messed-up individual, but he did not care as long as he got what he wanted. Nothing or no one else mattered.

Dana was in the kitchen cutting up the rest of the steak she grilled for dinner. Since Nate woke her up, she would eat some breakfast. Nate entered the kitchen while she was chopping up what seemed to be ingredients for an omelet. He walked over to the pantry to get a glass and he brushed up against her feeling the softness of her buttocks. Dana stiffened as he reached over her head to get a glass and then shut the pantry door. He went to the refrigerator to get something to drink then sat down at the table and just looked at her as she moved around the kitchen getting everything she needed to finish cooking.

Dana could feel Nate's eyes watching her. She thought about how his watching her use to make her feel. Now all she could feel was discomfort and disgust with him around. She did not want to feel anything for him and why should she? Everything about him made her sick to her stomach. He played with everything that she held sacred, her vows to him, her heart for him and her life with him. She had been hurt before, but this time it was different. She had never felt like a prisoner locked away with no one to lean on and no one to trust. He had taken her dignity, her heart, and everything she believed in for the sake of love and it got her nowhere. She would not allow herself to go through this again with any man. She would not allow him the satisfaction of taking her there. He nor anyone else would hold that power over her again!

When she finished cooking breakfast, she fixed him a plate and took hers to the living room to watch TV. He looked at her as she left the kitchen but said nothing. She was watching a movie when he came in to join her. She was still feeling a little tired from getting up so early, but she did not want to go upstairs to get into bed, so she finished eating her breakfast, took her plate to the kitchen, walked back to the living room and laid on the sofa to finish her movie. She was aware of his presence the whole time. She could feel where he sat and how he watched her. She tried to stay as still as possible but being uncomfortable made it impossible. She tried to concentrate on the movie she was watching. Every scene became cloudier as her eyelids grew heavier and heavier, then she fell asleep.

Nate watched her for a long time as she slept. He watched the slight little movements that she made, the moans and mumbles under her breath as if she was having an unpleasant dream one minute then a sensual one the next.

The sofa looked as if it was swallowing her up in it. He remembered the first time they made love on it, how it fit the two of them on it comfortably. He got up from where he was sitting and went over to the sofa where Dana laid and lay beside her. She did not budge when he touched her. He put his arm around her and went to sleep. Dana dreamed of the times when having peace of mind meant something good, when being free accounted for something. She wanted that feeling back. She had to have it.

Dreams of Nate invaded her senses. The arguments, the abuse, the smell of his cologne, the touch and feel of his hands the smile on his face, the way it felt when she lay in his arms as they spooned together, she could feel the warmth of it all in her dreams.

She dreamed of his warm breath on her neck

and the wetness of his tongue as it traveled down to her throat, her breast, her stomach and the center between her legs where he sucked and licked and bought her to such erotic climaxes. She sucked in her breath thinking she was still dreaming as she felt his hands caress her legs and buttocks while he worked his tongue around her clitoris. Her body arched up to him giving him access to invade her while he licked her slowly and softly, making her wetter and wetter. She opened her legs wider inviting him to suck her and lick her more freely. She could feel her body tense up as she felt the explosion coming closer, then with one violent shake of her body she was releasing into his mouth. She twisted, turned and shook until her body gave up every bit of stress and raw emotion it had to give. When it stopped, she laid limp on the sofa, trying to calm her breath, feeling dizzy and wanting more, yet at the same time hating him.

When she opened her eyes, she realized it had not been a dream at all, but Nate was right there at that moment. Dana saw the smoldering look in his eyes as he looked down at her. He was now on top of her and he was waiting for her to say no, but to say no at this point would end up in something she was not quite ready for. Anyway, it was too late now, she had gone too far already, and she wanted more. He entered her with a fierce thrust that sent Dana over the edge. He sexed her with fast angry strokes as if he was using something to hurt her with and not his manhood and she enjoyed every minute of it. He did not hurt her. She needed to be sexed this way. She too had a lot to get out of her system and with every thrust he gave her it took her closer and closer until she erupted like a volcano.

He collapsed on top of her and she went completely limp. They laid like that for what seemed to be hours. They fell asleep that way.

Dana woke to the sound of jazz playing on the stereo and the smell of something cooking. It smelled great and for a brief moment the thought of earlier played across her mind.

She felt relaxed and was content to lay on the sofa as she was completely naked. The CD he was playing was Four Play, one of her favorite jazz groups. When he came into the living room and noticed she was awake he smiled at her. He too was naked. It startled her to see him like this. It had been a long time. He went over to the bar, poured her a glass of wine and handed it to her. She looked at him with confused eyes and he gave a little snicker.

"Don't look at me like that," he told her.

"Like what?" Dana answered.

"Like a piece of shit," was Nate's response. Suddenly he looked alarmed and she held her breath. He turned and rushed back into the kitchen. When he returned, he brought out grilled Portobello's stuffed with crab meat and a salad tossed with shrimp. Dana looked at him for a moment then her smiled dropped. He eyed when he saw the drastic change in her features. Growing nervous now, Dana came back to reality knowing that this was not going to end well after that statement.

What was Nate up to? Why was he being so nice all of a sudden? How did he go from *you have another man* to having sex with her then cooking dinner? She took a breath and tried calming down as she eyed him suspiciously. She took a swallow of her wine, then another.

Nate saw her nervousness and put the plates down on the table to try and ease her tension. "Dana you have to eat, okay? We might as well enjoy what's left of the day seeing as it's almost over."

Dana looked surprised. "What do you mean almost over?"

He pointed to the window. She looked up and then at the clock, six in the evening. She slept all day. That never happens. *What happened,* she thought, then remembered the events that led up to now.

She cursed to herself aware that Nate was looking at her. Still a little tense, she took the plate and began to eat her food. They ate in silence, not saying a word to one another but occasionally exchanging glances. The sound of the music relaxed her little by little as she took all of this in. It was Nate who broke the silence. "Would you like another the glass of wine?"

"Yes," she answered him.

CHAPTER TWELVE

The food was good, but she did not have too much of an appetite. She was wondering what he was up to. She put her plate down on the table.

"Why are you being nice to me?" she asked Nate.

"Why are you messing up a good thing?" he responded.

She looked at him weary of their entire situation then answered, "I'm not Nate, you are!"

She was tired of this sick and twisted game he was playing with her. What did he wish to accomplish? She wanted to ask but decided not to.

"Look Dana, I'm home. Could you just leave it at that?"

Nate tried not to get impatient with her, he saw the agitation in her eyes, and he did not want it to get out of hand. He noticed a difference about her, an almost nonchalance about her. Her eyes did not shine the way they had before he married her, he knew he had given her reason to be this way, but he did not care. He saw how other men looked at her and how everyone took to her immediately. She had what every man wanted. Looks, intelligence, personality, great sex and she could cook. So why was he like this with her? he kept asking himself. *Because she is everything my mother said a female was not,* he thought to himself.

Dana got up from the sofa, "I am going upstairs to take a shower." Then she left the room and walked upstairs.

He watched her as she walked from living room to the hallway. He knew he had hurt her, but this was not about her. It was about him and what he wanted. He was not about to let any female tell him what to do or lock him down. Hell, all this free ass in the world and he was supposed to stop being him because he said, "I do?" He had made his mother a promise and damn it he was going to stick to it.

He got up out of the chair he was sitting in and poured another glass of wine, this time he put something in it, something that was going to make this night the way he wanted it. He popped a pill and swallowed it down with some wine, picked up the glass and walked upstairs.

Dana was in the shower when Nate walked in the room. He sat down the wine and waited for her to be through taking her shower. He did not have to wait long. She was turning off the water and drying herself off not even minutes after he came into the room. He turned on the intercom in the room to reflect the music playing down stairs.

When she walked into the room, he was sitting on the bed smiling at her. Her heart raced as she remembered that smile from long ago, but knew it was nothing more than a game he played to toy with her emotions. He got up from where he was sitting and handed her the glass of wine.

"Relax," he told her. "This is a friendly gesture

towards a truce, and you were so good earlier that it made me want to finish this day out."

Dana took the wine but still felt a certain suspicion towards Nate.

"Dana, I know you have needs, hell everybody does and before I let anyone else take care of them, I'll be the one to do it. Understand now, you belong to me and that means I can do whatever I want to you anytime I want to do it."

Dana listened to him as he spoke; his movements were slow and intent as if he was a panther about to attack his prey. She took another sip of her wine, the liquid felt warm as it went down her throat. She took another sip of the liquid then noticed how unusually relaxed she was. Almost as if she was dreaming. The closer he got to her the more she wanted him near her. She could feel her body reacting to his every step; unusual warmth took over and her senses whirled. She could feel the juices stir in her body down below for him and she had no power to stop herself from feeling this way.

"Do you know why you can't leave me Dana?" Nate asked her. "Because if you did, no man would ever be able to touch you like I touch you." His hands caressed and teased her body not leaving a single spot untouched as he spoke to her. "Nor will you be able to respond to any man the way I can make you respond to me," he taunted her as he whispered in her ear.

A single tear ran down her face as she tried to say something, anything, but the more she tried the more it seemed impossible. Dana felt as if she was paralyzed. Her legs felt heavy. She tried to will herself to move, but the more she tried the harder it was. Her body felt like it was on fire and she could feel perspiration swell up. Just then, Nate picked her up off of her feet, her lifeless body succumbing to his every move as he carried her over to the bed. Her body went limp as he laid her down. He did not bother to pull the covers back. Nate climbed on top of her and he noticed another single tear come from her eye and roll down her cheek.

He whispered in her ear, "Why the tears? I'm giving you what you want Dana. Tell me what you want," he said to her as his tongue ran down her body. "Is it this?" he asked again as he went to the center between her legs taunting and teasing her. "Or is it this?"

She gasped for air as he licked her, softly playing with the little thing that protruded from the middle between her legs. Her senses were heightened from the sheer feel of it all. *He has surely lost his mind* she thought. The abuse was one thing but drugging her was another. She tried to speak but no words came out of her mouth. She tried to breathe but it was almost impossible. She tried to move her body, but to no avail. She felt like someone poured cement all over her, making it impossible for her to move at all. The only thing she could do was feel everything he was doing to her sexually aching body, making her want everything he was doing to her without being able to fight against it and hating him for making her feel this way all at the same time. Making, every part of her body want and need every inch and touch.

He had tricked her into wanting him, needing him. She wanted to scream. She felt helpless. This was torture. He was tormenting her like only he could. She thought and at that moment she realized he could kill her and their wouldn't be anything she could do about it.

Later that night Dana woke up feeling something cold rubbing down her leg, she opened her eyes and noticed Nate had a gun in his hands. Dana stiffened with fear still feeling a little groggy from whatever Nate used on her earlier. Nate took the weapon and inserted it into her vagina.

"Dana," he whispered. Dana was scared to answer him. "Do you feel this?" he asked her.

She nodded, scared to do anything else. Know that I will pull the trigger," he told her. Dana felt the blood drain from her body. Nate saw the fear in her and he smiled. He knew he had her right where he wanted her.

He dared her to move and she was too afraid to. He dared her to scream and again she was afraid to.

"You know if I pull the trigger right now, I could clean up your mess and get away with it? I did it once and I'll do it again; get away with it I mean."

Dana's heart pounded and she felt as if she would pass out. The look in his eyes made her feel that if she made one wrong move that would be the end of her. She had never in her life seen death this close and she knew that her life depended on her not making a wrong move. She also knew that if she had to choose which one of them would live, she would choose herself to walk out of this alive. She prayed very quietly to herself where he could not hear her.

Father I come to you in a time of fear and desperation. Please put my enemy under your feet. Shield me with a hedge and a wall of protection all around me. Take this darkness from around me and replace it with your glorious light. My time is in your hands. Thank you for being in complete control of my life. In Jesus name.

Dana was glad to be back at work. It had been weeks since that frightening experience with Nate had happened.

She needed an outlet and being at work was what she needed for now. Since that night Nate had been doing him, as usual. Being at home when he wanted which was a little more than usual. He was trying to keep tabs on her more as well. They did not talk much, just the occasional hi and bye sort of thing. They had not had sex since that night either which was alright with her. He had violated her in every way he could, trying to break her, but Dana refused to be broken. She could not stand the sight of him and it made her feel sick to be around him. All she had was her job to make her feel good about herself, for now.

She remembered when she told him she was going back to work. He nodded at her then told her he would be watching her. She was just glad to be doing something that took her mind off of him and their joke of a marriage. The phone in her office rang. It was her boss calling to tell her that he needed her to meet with the contractors for the new location in Florida. She was more than happy to do it. Even happier that they were opening up a restaurant there.

She always wanted to live in a house by the water or close to it. Sunshine, the beach, palm trees much different from Atlanta, where she lived now, and she would get to be with her son Eric. They wanted her to be in charge down there seeing that she was vital to their success here and knowing what she was going through in her present situation. She had planned to leave them soon, but the new turn of events worked in her favor. She had a lot of catching up to do at work. The owners did what they could do in her absence, but they did not have the same system she did.

It was seven o'clock when she decided to leave and before she could get into her car good her phone was ringing. Nate had made it a point to call her daily to make sure she made it home whether he would be there or not. He even stopped by to check up on her. No one liked him on the job. They were always ready to beat the heck out of him but treated him with respect every time he walked through the door. They took the ban off him entering the store so that Dana could continue to work for them. Dana had not told him about the new restaurant opening up in Florida. It would mess up all the plans she had made for herself.

A new life she thought, she had been hopeful and excited about her new life away from Nate. She needed a new beginning. This last two years were a nightmare and she promised herself that she would not let any man control or manipulate her again. Love was no longer an option for Dana, not now and not ever!

"I'm going home," Nate told the other woman.

"Why," the other woman asked him now angry.

"Do you think you can just use me and sex me any time you want to then go back home to your wife?" she asked him. "Who in the hell do you think you are? I won't stand for this Nate!" the other woman yelled to the top of her voice.

Nate looked at her and answered, "Then don't." The other woman looked at him, her eyes narrowed at the response she got. She looked away from him out of the car window, "Okay Nate, I won't! Do not call me anymore for anything!"

She seethed, Nate turned around with a swift move to look at the woman sitting next to him.

The woman flinched, fearful of what he would do to her.

"Let's get one thing straight hoe! I don't need you for nothing remember that! The only thing you can do for me is blow me when I ask you to."

She looked at him with surprise in her eyes. "And let me fill you in on another thing trick; you are married too. The only reason you have so much free time on your hands is because your husband chooses to be with someone much younger than you, in an apartment you furnished for his other woman!" he spat out venom when he spoke.

"So what?" the woman screamed. "Look at you, you have a wife at home that you treat like shit. Not to mention you're always with me, your other woman, who by the way put you up in an apartment to get away from that bitch you call a wife. She is better than me, because I would not take the shit she puts up with!" she spat out in defense.

This time Nate slapped the woman in the face then he wrapped his hands around her neck. "You are a stupid hoe lady. You are taking it and from both sides. You've allowed yourself to be the other woman with your husband and with me so who's the stupid bitch now?" he hissed. "The only difference between me and your husband is I have eye candy with a damn good piece of ass at home," he said between his teeth. "The only thing he has is you when he walks through the door, and that's not saying much!"

He let her go and turned to open the door.

"What about when we're having sex?" she asked him in a hurtful voice.

He looked around at the other woman then responded, "What about it?" Then he turned away, opened the car door and left, slamming the door behind him.

"Nate!" the other woman screamed his name, but he did not turn to answer her.

Women, Nate thought. *What made her think he would be faithful to her and he wasn't even faithful*

103

to home. He can get a piece of ass when he couldn't get anything to eat and he was never hungry!

CHAPTER THIRTEEN

Dana was already home when Nate came in. He looked at her said nothing then went upstairs to take a shower. Okay, she thought that was her queue to be silent for the rest of the night. Not that they talked anyway which made it all the better. Dana was out back when Nate came back downstairs. He was agitated and whatever it was, it was not her business. She had mixed up some hamburger while he was upstairs bathing.

"What are we having for dinner he asked her?" Dana sat back in her seat with a glass of wine in her hand.

"I made hamburger patties, started the grill up and was waiting for you to work your magic." She tried to make light of the attitude he had. "You also have some beer in the fridge, wanted to get them cold for you so I put a couple in the freezer.

He looked at her as if she was up to something then he frowned, "Okay what gives?" he asked her still looking at her.

"Nothing," she answered not looking his way. "You came in the door and went upstairs, I put a couple of beers in the freezer for you and made some hamburger patties. Did I do something wrong?"

He grunted, turned away from her and walked in

the house, but not before he said, "Smart ass."

Dana did not respond but thought to herself *whatever made him angry did a good job at it. Must be trouble in paradise, she shook her head.* She sighed to herself and thought *this is going to be an early night for me.* She took another sip of wine and thought, *I have never in my life drank this much but then again, I like wine.*

The next couple of weeks went by like a blur; there was so much to do with the planning of the restaurant.

The owners were in and out of town frequently making sure the plans and design was going like they wanted. It was due to open in about three weeks and she was excited and scared at the same time. That night that Nate came home peed off, he tried to argue with her about her reading a book.

When she did not fall for it, he started slamming doors, and throwing things, one of them being her phone again, but not before he went through it. He yelled at her and called her a stupid bitch. When Dana did not respond to him and his antics and walked away from him, he followed her upstairs and slapped her calling her an insensitive hoe. Needless to say, she went to bed fearful that if she did retaliate, she would once again feel a gun entering her which sacred her. She thought about how it would be not to go through this abuse with Nate and with the month almost up and the grand opening of the restaurant coming up she had thought of that single moment when she would leave and never look back. She looked up to the sky and took a deep breath.

Dana got off work early, she was not feeling well, but before she left, she made sure everything was done and running right.

She had made a visit to all of the stores early that morning and made calls to different vendors, collected all the invoices she needed and completed her work in a timely fashion, now she was driving home or to the house she occupied at this time, she thought as she pulled up in the driveway, got out of her car and went into the house.

She was changing her clothes when she heard the doorbell ring downstairs. She ran down to answer and when she opened the door the other woman was standing on the other side. She looked Dana up and down before she asked, "Is Nate here?" Dana looked at the other woman before something in her clicked. She pushed the woman out of her doorway.

"Nate, is not here and if he was, I still would not get him for you, now get the hell away from my door before I catch a case for killing you."

The woman's eyes opened wider then she said, "His mother was right about you, you think you're all that, you think you got him, but you don't. Do you know that every time you give him head you taste my juices all over him?"

Dana smiled at the other woman but deep inside wanted to kick this bitch's ass for coming to her door with this bullshit, but instead she said, "Excuse me, but my husband told me that giving blow jobs was for nasty hoes only! That's why you have that job!" then she slammed the door in the woman's face. Dana could not believe the nerve of this woman coming to her door, *so desperate that she would have the gall to disrespect another woman's house*! "Crazy, trifling ass people!" she screamed from the top of her lungs.

It started to get dark outside and all was quiet in the house, at least that was what Dana thought. Not a minute passed after she thought it was safe that she heard Nate opening the door, but not only that he had brought company with him. Dana's eyes widened in astonishment. It was the other woman. Nate watched her response as he walked in the door. "Dana this is Liz."

Dana could not believe what was happening. Had he lost his mind bringing her here? Dana looked at the other woman like a disease. "How dare you walk into another woman's house knowing she knows you are sleeping with her husband!" Dana responded. "Why is she here?"

"She wanted to see the inside of the house, so I'm showing her."

"Show her!" Dana said. "Did she tell you she was already here looking for you? That I had to push her out of the doorway?" *This was crazy,* Dana thought. *Who does this kind of thing?*

"Did you not know I would be here or is this some sick joke on your behalf?" Dana spat back. Not caring what happened next, she looked at the woman and told her to get out. The woman looked at her and said, "Only if Nate wants me to leave."

Then she looked at Nate.

With both women standing there watching him Nate told the woman to sit down. She looked at Dana like she won a tournament of some sort, then obeyed Nate and took a seat.

"Fine Nate, if you don't want her to leave then I'll leave, no problem. Move her in so you can fight with her. I'm done and over it."

Dana was furious now. She left the room, went upstairs and started packing her clothes. Nate followed her grabbed on to her arm and shouted, "I told you, you're not going anywhere unless it's in a body bag!"

Dana looked at Nate then responded, "Fine Nate, then in a body bag it will be!" she spat out. He hesitated for a moment before he spoke another word.

"This is my house and I can bring whoever I want in here."

Everything was moving so fast. Her mind was going a mile a second, but one thing she knew and that was she would not go through this another day. Secondly, she knew that one of them tonight was definitely leaving whether it was in a body bag or not.

Nate entered into the room running toward Dana and some kind of way Dana managed to push up against him with everything she had, and he hit the floor before she knew it. With a look of rage Nate got up off the floor, he ran towards her and pushed her down.

The other woman hearing everything that was

going on upstairs got up from the couch nervously and walked towards the stairs, she called his name from downstairs. Hearing this, he told her to go home, he'd call her later. She called his name again.

"Go home!" he yelled, then the door slammed. He went back in the room, but then the horn beeped and beeped again. Nate cursed under his breath, then looked at Dana. He then left the room running downstairs and slamming the door behind him.

How could this happen to her? Dana felt as if her heart had been ripped opened by a knife. Her head pounding and racing at the same time, she knew she had to get out no matter what. She was no longer safe in her own home anymore. How could she let things get this far? She knew he would never let her leave without a fight. She could feel her heart beating as she tried to think things out, her adrenaline was pumping at such a rate she felt dizzy and she looked around the room to see if she could find something, anything to defend herself with, but then she heard the door open and close.

Her breathing quickened and once again Nate was there. He ran upstairs taking two at a time, all of a sudden there was a loud crash and a series of thumps. Dana jumped from the sounds. She ran to the stairs to see that he had fallen back down the stairs. Dana ran back to the room to look for the car keys. She spotted them on the dresser, so she picked them up and turned to run out of the room. When she saw him coming in the room, he approached Dana swinging at her. She ducked to keep from getting hit and lost her balance. She fell to the floor. He kicked her in the stomach, she gasped for air coughing then he slammed her head on the floor over and over, Dana could see nothing but darkness.

Just then, Nate told her, "I meant what I said Dana. You're not going anywhere."

Fuming now, Dana tried to jerk away from him, but his grip tightened around her arm as she fought against him and he pushed her away from him. Dana's mind was racing, and throbbing and she was so angry she could not think straight. Now how could he have brought this female in her house, their house, leave her downstairs then come up here to fight with his wife? Right then she felt a sharp pain in her head. He put his hands around her throat and squeezed. She gasped for air and for a moment she thought she was dreaming. Then all of a sudden, she felt something warm dripping down her forehead and then it grew silent, with her own breath shallow. Dana slipped into unconsciousness.

Nate shook her trying to wake her up, but she did not move not at all. He paced back and forth trying to get his lie straight before he called the paramedics. He looked at Dana again, still there was no movement.

Nate took a deep breath to get his mind together before he made the call. He looked down at Dana, she didn't make a move and he saw the blood coming from her head and swore to himself. Then he made the call. "Hello 911 it's my wife, she had an accident can you please send someone now?" he spoke frantically in the phone.

CHAPTER FOURTEEN

When Dana opened her eyes, she was lying in a different bed in a different room. Her vision was blurred, but she could see people around her. There was a lot of movement around her. She tried to say something but then she drifted off again. It was about two hours later when she fluttered her eyes open to try and see better, but everything was still foggy. She could hear someone speaking with a male voice.

"Mrs. Johnson, can you hear me? This is doctor..." but she drifted off again, before she heard his name. When Dana finally opened her eyes again, the last thing she remembered was the doctor trying to tell her his name, but what was she doing at the hospital? Then the argument with Nate came back to her. The doctor was entering the room at the same time that everything came back to her.

"Hello Mrs. Johnson. You gave us a fright. You were out for a while, we were wondering when you were going to come back to us."

"Come back to you?" Dana looked around the room and saw Nate sitting beside her bed watching her.

"You received a nasty bump on your head, and you needed some stitches," the doctor had a worried look on his face as he filled her in. He looked at Nate then back at Dana. "We're going to keep you a day or two for observation, just to make sure everything is okay before we release you, standard procedure."

Dana nodded.

"If I can, I would like to ask you some questions about what happened today."

Dana licked her lips, looked at the doctor then at Nate before she said, "Everything is a little foggy and my head hurts, can we do this some other time?"

The doctor noticed her reaction. He was watching her more intently now. He waited for a minute before answering, "Yes, that's fine. In the meantime, I'll have the nurse give you some pain medicine to help you sleep and we'll talk more tomorrow. Mr. Johnson, I am going to ask you to leave so that my patient can get some rest tonight. She's in good hands now."

Nate looked at the other man with suspicion before answering, "Sure, yes. Just let me have a word with my wife before I leave."

The doctor answered as he was leaving, "Yes, of course. I'll give you two some privacy." But he did not go far.

Nate got close to Dana like he was going to kiss her but instead he whispered to her. "Remember what I told you Dana, I will kill you and I swear I mean every word of it." He kissed her on the forehead while the nurse was coming into the room. He turned around and added, "Oh," he said, "I'll let Eric know that his mother is doing fine. Goodnight babe see you in the morning," then he was gone.

Dana blew out a sigh of relief when he left. Then all of a sudden, she thought about what he said about Eric. Her eyes widened. What did he mean he would let Eric know? She grew agitated.

The nurse drew out the needle and was getting ready to put its contents of the medicine in her IV when the doctor came back in the room. "Hold on just a minute nurse, let me have a few words with our patient here."

The nurse nodded, then started to leave, but the doctor stopped her. "Nurse Kelly, I need you to stay while I ask Mrs. Johnson a few questions."

The nurse nodded in response then stayed as asked.

"Mrs. Johnson, I noticed upon your arrival some very unusual bruises around your neck not to mention a very nasty blows to your head. Can you tell me how you got them?"

Dana blinked her eyes in nervousness her eyes growing big at the question. The doctor patted her arm lightly, "Don't worry, I made sure your husband left the hospital. I have grown daughters myself and if I thought their husbands had hurt and abused them in any way I would have them arrested if I did not kill them first." He smiled at her, and tears ran down her face.

"Nurse Kelly, the doctor said in an stern but soft voice, the nurse immediately turned to him in response, "call the police."

Dana was lying in the bed when the police arrived, a female and a man. They asked her to tell them everything that happened. Dana's mouth was dry, but she told them everything they wanted to know.

It seemed like it took forever but she told them everything she could think of, every sorted detail.

The female officer took pictures of all her bruises, the officers did everything they could to reassure her that she was safe and in good hands then she asked them to do her one last favor.

The officer answered her, "We'll try. What do you need?"

"Can you call and check on my son Eric? He lives in Florida with his grandparents. The phone number is 904-555-7798, explain to them what's happened. They will know how to handle it from there."

"We sure will ma'am and we will get back to you as soon as we do," he reassured her.

She smiled at the officers, "Can you wait until he comes here in the morning to arrest him?" she asked them.

The officers looked at one another. "Why in the morning ma'am?" they asked.

"If you go to the house now you won't catch him, but if you wait until the morning, I know that I will be safe enough to go home, pack my clothes, and leave town. How long will he be in jail for?" she asked the officers.

"Well with the pictures we have of your bruises along with the death threats and not to mention the statement you gave us; the judge is not going to let him out right away."

"Do you know if he has a record?" they asked

her.

"I'm not sure."

The officer asked her, "How long do you need ma'am?"

She thought for a minute then she answered, "A week at least."

Both officers looked at one another and nodded their heads as if they were talking in code. "We'll post a couple of officers on this floor ma'am and will advise the staff that when he comes in the morning to let the officers on duty know. We'll pick him up before he gets the chance to come in here." Dana looked up at the doctor and he squeezed her arm to reassure her that she had nothing to worry about. When the officers left the room, the doctor gave the nurse permission to give Dana the pain medicine. Then he informed the nurses station to call him if he wasn't already there so that he could be there for Dana in the morning.

Dana was so exhausted that she went right to sleep, sleeping as if she had not slept in a decade. The next morning Dana woke to loud noise coming from the hallway. She could hear the officers and she could hear Nate calling her name. She laid in silence, too scared to move and too scared to speak.

The doctor came in and walked around to where she was, letting her know she had nothing to worry about. Dana heard some scuffling and people talking, then it went silent. Five minutes later an officer came in the room to brief her on the events taking place.

"Ma'am we have just arrested your husband for

assault, domestic violence with the intent of doing bodily harm and resisting arrest. We have him secured in the vehicle, and if we have any more questions, we know how to get in touch with you. Be assured that you are safe now."

Then he patted her on the arm. It was the same officer from last night. He smiled at her and asked, "Do you know when you are to be released?"

The doctor answered, "Tomorrow."

The officer nodded at her. I also would like to inform you that we contacted your son's grandparents and they reassured us that he's safe and doing well." Then he wished her good luck. Before he left out of the room he turned back around and told her, "Ma'am you are one of the lucky ones. Not everyone makes it out of an abusive situation safely or alive." He then turned and left the room.

Dana laid back in the bed breathing a sigh of relief for the first time in ages. It was over. No more physical abuse, no more women calling her house thinking she was his aunt, no more mental abuse, no more cheating, no more lies. Tears streamed down her face uncontrollably as she thought of a new life without bondage. She was happier than she had been in a long time. She was finally free in every sense of the word and she would not look back.

Dana looked at the clock on the nightstand. It was four am. This was the third time this month she had awakened to a dream. She got out of bed and went downstairs to the kitchen. The dreams she had been having were different every time. She could hear the gun going off. She could feel her body burning, and she could feel her body going limp, then she would wake up. Dana had been in Florida for a year now and she loved it there. She had a three-bedroom house with a large eat in kitchen that opened out into the living room. There was a pool in the back with a screened in patio, three large bedrooms and peace of mind that made it that much more wonderful. Everything about Florida was great, so great she could go to the beach anytime she liked.

She and Eric went often. The weather was always warm and that she liked very much. The owners of the restaurant visited her frequently. They gave her a couple of months to enjoy her new environment and to get her life back on track. They knew what she went through in Georgia and they did not want to lose her. She had been the biggest reason why their business was such a success in the first place. They made it a point to stop by every time they were in town to check in on she and Eric. They had grown attached to them both, so attached they considered them their own.

Though she was not physically working at the moment, she was in constant contact with the contractors and vendors whenever they needed to ask any questions. They also gave her time off with pay which really helped her out even though she had a nest egg. She was finally free from a life of turmoil, confusion and abuse. That part of her life was over, and she would never let herself be controlled by anyone ever again. Her focus was on living and enjoying life to the fullest and having a relationship of any kind was not a thought nor an option and that suited her just fine. She also wanted to make sure that everything was super safe before she moved Eric in with her. She wanted him to be safe.

Dana made arrangements to move her son Eric in as soon as possible. His grandparents were sad to see him go but were happy that he and his mother would be together in the same house and in the same state. Now they would have two for the price of one and that made them much more happy. Eric's father was their only son. He had been killed in action in Iraq and he and Dana were not together when he passed. They had broken up when Eric was one. The relationship they had lasted only a year. He had been so stuck on his parent's money that making his own was out of the equation. He thought that if they were well off, he was too. He thought they owed it to him. He did not understand that they worked hard for what they had. He was always putting Dana down, telling her things like "You need to feel honored and privileged to sit in my car," and, "you should feel special being in my presence." One time he told her, "You don't cook like my mother, you need to call her for lessons." Dana was appalled when he told her that, seeing that she came from a long line of women who could throw down when it came to cooking. After hearing him give himself the glory, Dana got fed up and ended it.

Dana grew up in a house where both of her parents worked, and they worked hard. They made decent money. Her father was a postal worker and her mother worked for a well-known bank as a bank manager. One of the things they taught her was to never forget who you are and where you came from.

That's why she never judged anyone for what they had or what they could give her as long as they worked hard for what they had. People come from many walks of life and you never know what a person is going through in life or what they have been through, that's why you don't judge anyone unfairly.

She was happy to be reunited with him. She didn't know what she would do if something ever happened to him. She would keep him hidden from the world if she could. She would do whatever she had to do to keep him safe. She thought of Nate and took a deep breath and a sigh of relief.

"Thank you, Father, for delivering me from the hand of evil. Thank you for your grace. In Jesus name."

CHAPTER FIFTEEN

Dana was not finished furnishing her house. She wanted to take her time so that when it was all complete, she could enjoy her home all the more. She wanted her son's room to be the bedroom that young boys dreamed about so off shopping she went. She purchased him a bedroom set that every boy his age would appreciate; pure oak with the drawers made into the bed, a chest of drawer and a nightstand. She also purchased a desk and a computer to do his school work so he could keep his grades up. She picked out colors that she thought a boy of his age would like, accessories and the works. Satisfied with everything, she went home to decorate.

Since she had been in Florida Eric had only come with her on the weekends. Although she had the freedom and peace, she wanted to be absolutely sure he would be safe and free from harm, she had not heard a word from or about Nate since she left Georgia behind. That was fine with her. She was home with her son and now she would have him for good. That made her very happy!

Eric woke to the sound of his mother's voice on several occasions. He'd been home now for five months and he enjoyed the time he got to spend with his mother. He could tell something was not right because a lot lately he could hear his mother screaming at night. It woke him each time and when it did, he would get out of bed and walk to her room only to be told, "I'm alright it was just a bad dream, go back to bed."

His eyebrows would crinkle but he would do as he was told. One night he went to the kitchen and made her some warm milk. It always seemed to work when his grandma use to do it for him. When he took it to her room she was sitting up in her bed, holding her pillow and rocking back and forth. He startled her when he called her name.

"Mama?"

"Yes sweetie?" she answered him.

"I made you some warm milk, don't worry I didn't mess with the stove, I used the microwave instead."

She smiled at him and told him to come and sit by her. She took the milk and drank some, even though she did not like milk. She did not want to hurt his feelings knowing that he did it to make her feel better. Eric was looking at her drink the milk.

He gave her a thumbs up and smiled with satisfaction that he did a good deed then he said to her "Don't worry mom I'll protect you, I won't let anything bad happen to you ever."

Dana put her milk down on the nightstand beside her and hugged her son. She thanked him for her milk then she told him that she was fine, and he could go back to bed. Eric kissed his mother on the cheek and did as he was told, only turning to say, "I love you mama, sweet dreams," on his way out the door.

He did not see the tears rolling down her face because the lights were out when she responded, "Mom loves you too sweetheart."

Eric was a mild-mannered boy who did everything his mother asked him to do. Even though he liked going outside playing with the other kids he still kept to himself some of the time. His mother sent him to a private school at the age of eight. She wanted to give him what she did not have. A chance to see the world, to experience different cultures, meet new people, to learn and see things with a broader perspective and she knew sending him to one of the best schools in Florida would provide that. Eric was a straight A student and even though he had the best education that anyone could ever have, he missed his mother dearly. He missed the time they use to spend together, how they celebrated the holidays and how just being around her made him feel happy. Sure, he still got the chance to see her and spend time with her, but it was nothing like how it had been, not since she got the job in Atlanta, but now things would change. She was here now, and he saw her everyday now since he lived with her, but something had changed about her. She still was the fun person she always was, but now she had a sad look. She was so jumpy now and she was always turning around like she was looking for somebody.

Eric knew something was wrong when one day he heard her and grandma talking about that bad man. Grandma said she had done the right thing getting away from him, and that he could not hurt her anymore, Eric got upset when he heard this. They did not know that he had heard them talking. One night before Eric got into bed, he got his baseball bat out of the corner of his closet and got on his knees and prayed.

"Dear Lord, help me to protect my mom from the bad man. I want her to be happy all the time and not sad. Thank you and I love you. Amen"

He got into bed putting his bat underneath the covers beside him. "Don't worry mom," he said. "I have my bat beside me, so he won't hurt you anymore!" Then he closed his eyes and went to sleep.

Time passed and Eric was happier than he had ever been. Mama even seemed to be better. He did not hear her scream like before. She did work a lot, but she made up for it by spending time with him every chance she got.

His grandparents looked after him now that Dana was back at work, she took him to school, and they pick him up.

On her days off she let him pick what they're going to do for the day. Surprisingly enough Eric always pick pizza and the pool. He loved swimming and she loved spending time with him. Dana had not realized just how much she had missed her son. Just being around him and talking to him made her almost forget what she had gone through in Georgia.

The owners of the restaurant came by today

unexpectedly. They usually called her first, but she did not worry, they were always welcomed, they had become family as far as she was concerned. Anyway, all was well, and everything was going great at the restaurant. Dana actually used this as a home base while she oversaw the planning and building of the other four restaurants.

"Dana!" Julia hugged her "We miss you in Atlanta, but we could not be happier that you're here taking care of things." As they exchanged hugs, Dana could not help but notice the man standing next to them. Julia continued, "John and I would like you to meet our latest addition to our restaurant family!" Dana looked surprised as she repeated "addition" while looking at this mysterious man.

"Yes" Julia exclaimed, this is Vernon Cruze."

She put her hand out to shake his hand and he did the same. "Nice to meet you," she told him.

He smiled at her then responded, "Likewise." He had the firmest handshake, but the softest hands and when he smiled his eyes lit up. Their eyes locked for a brief moment and it was Dana who spoke first as she turned her attention back to Julia.

"You said addition, what will you be doing Mr. Cruze?" she asked. Julia chimed in, "Well dear, since we are opening up four new restaurants with two more in the planning stage, Vernon will be helping you."

Dana stared at the older woman. "Helping me?" Dana sounded alarmed at the idea. "What do you mean helping me? I can handle this on my own, I don't need any help."

The mysterious man just smiled at her, aware that she had not taken her eyes off of him the whole time he was standing there. Julia cut in

"No dear, I don't want you to think we feel you can't handle it. We know better than that. We know that Eric lives with you now and to keep you from having to travel so much and stay away so long we brought someone who is not attached to anyone. He has no distractions in his life, no wife and his children are all grown up."

Dana looked at Julia with a frustrated look and she saw something like a snicker coming from Julia, *so she thinks this is funny!*

Dana looked at the stranger then at John, Julia's husband, then back at Julia. Dana, not thinking any of this was humorous in the least bit, held her head up, stiffened her back and asked, "Okay when does he start?"

Julia blew out a sigh of relief and was pleased that Dana agreed with them. She said, "We'll all go out to dinner and talk about everything."

Dana, now aggravated with Julia, replied, "Fine, when?"

Ecstatic and humored by Dana's reaction to all of this, Julia clapped her hands in excitement.

"What about tonight say around seven?"

"Fine," Dana answered before she walked way.

The mysterious stranger listening to the whole conversation never took his eyes off of Dana, not one time. She had the most beautiful brown eyes he had seen in a long time. Julia continued talking and he nodded at all that she was saying, but he was not really listening to her. All the while he could not get the picture out of his head of the beautiful woman that had just walked away.

Vernon Cruze was six two and had the complexion of milk chocolate. A tall, slender looking man with broad shoulders, strong muscular arms and a pair of gorgeous brown eyes, and when he smiled you had to hold your breath because of the deep dimples in his face.

"He has a degree in the culinary arts and a knack for business," Julia added in.

Julia and John had met him at a restaurant convention while he was there networking and researching all the business do's and don'ts for opening up his own restaurant. John and Julia liked him instantly. He was very intelligent, they thought, and would be good for what they had in mind so they made him a proposition of their own that he could not refuse. If he worked for them for two years helping out with the openings of their restaurants in Florida, they would in turn invest in his. Vernon liked those terms seeing that he made his living catering events; he made a decent living at it and had managed to save up a good little nest egg because of it. That's how he came up with the idea of opening his own establishment.

He was not married, although he had been at one time, that ended in divorce. He had two kids which were grown up and doing their own thing. He heard from them occasionally and tried to see them when they weren't busy with their own lives.

Having adult children had its ups and downs, and he only saw them when they made time for him.

At the restaurant they all discussed the planned jurisdictions for them both. They did not want Dana in the state of Georgia even though she had not been back since that tragic time. They wanted her to have say, but release some of the work to Vernon so that it didn't interfere with her and Eric's life and time with one another.

They all agreed that he had to report back to Dana even though he had the authority to do what he needed to do to make it happen. All the time he eyed her through dinner and the conversations. She was beautiful and she knew her stuff. He would make sure the work relationship would be like a hand in a glove, perfectly fitting.

Vernon was sitting in his living room and thought of Dana. He had found out a lot about her through John and Julia. She was smart in her business dealings, she definitely knew what she was talking about and how to make things happen. It's no wonder she worked for John and Julia. She knew her stuff, yet there was something about her almost broken. You could see it in her eyes as beautiful as they were, very beautiful indeed he thought, but frightened, angry and cold even when she tried to mask them by smiling.

He noticed at dinner how she kept it all business with the occasional smile that did not quite reach her eyes. She was definitely beautiful with a body to boot, but she had a barrier up so big it would take a person destroying mountains before she let them

129

down. He also noticed how she excused herself and bid everyone goodnight after everything was finalized. The rest of them stayed to have a nightcap.

When Julia told him the story of the last relationship Dana had been in, Vernon listened, but could not believe the ordeal she had gone through. The thought of it made him sick and he wanted to break the man's neck himself.

Some men are such cowards, he thought. *They don't want you, but they don't want anyone else to have you, so they try and break you. They beat and treat a woman like dirt all because they themselves don't know the true meaning of being a man, but if you catch them on the street alone, they would piss their pants being confronted man to man.*

Vernon grew more and more angry as he thought about what Dana had been through. Because of that sorry excuse of a man that had damaged her from ever wanting or having a loving and meaningful relationship with a man who could really show her what love and happiness could be.

Finishing his nightcap, Vernon thought of a time where protection was needed, and he wasn't there. He wouldn't let that happen again. Especially with Dana, she did something to him the first time he laid eyes on her. He would keep things professional, but he would make sure she could trust him with any and everything. He tossed the rest of his drink back and went to bed.

CHAPTER SIXTEEN

Dana lay in bed that night thinking about the changes getting ready to take place at work. She was happy that more of her time would be freed up so she could spend it with her son. She would be able to pick him up from school and be more involved when it came to his extracurricular activities. What she was not happy about was the frequent dealings with Vernon Cruze. Dana remembered how he looked at her and watched her. No matter what she did or said he was watching her, and she was aware of him. *He was fine* she had to admit to herself, but she felt like a frog being dissected by a biology teacher and that made her very uncomfortable.

When all discussions about the restaurant were finished, she excused herself and left them to be social. Even walking out of the restaurant, she could feel him watching her. It was unnerving and brought back feelings of a sexual desire that she had long forgotten. A desire that she could not partake in. She had been there, done that, and was never doing it again. She made herself a promise a long time ago not to trust or fall in love with anyone else and she meant it!

She got a chill that made her wince. Memories of a time past of being abused and cheated on. A time when love did not love her or want her, came flooding back with a picture of a face that still haunted her. She could not, would not let herself get involved with anyone. She would not let herself be controlled ever again.

"No!" She looked down at her hands. She broken out in a cold sweat and was trembling. It was the voice of her son Eric that brought her back to reality.

"Mom, how was dinner with Uncle John and Aunt Julia?"

"Huh?" she answered, as she forced herself to calm down, allowing the painful memories to disappear.

"Fine sweetie, they told me to tell you they will see you tomorrow. Now come give me a hug and go back to bed."

Eric hugged his mom then did as she asked. The next morning Dana woke up feeling refreshed, not thinking about anything but the future and what was in front of her. That did not involve anyone but her and her son. She got out of bed, then showered and thought about the day ahead of her. Dana felt freer than she'd ever felt, providing her a sense of peace and contentment with her life. She had just entered the kitchen when her phone rang.

"Hello?"

"Dana, how are you?"

She recognized Julia's voice on the other end. "I'm well, thank you," she responded. Still a little frustrated with the older lady but loving her like a mother anyway.

"I thought we could do something today like go to the beach, but seeing that it's dreadfully hot out, how about we come to your house and take a dip in the pool? I was thinking John could start the grill and whip us something up. We could make something tropical to drink and catch up on things. I promise no business talk, but you took off so suddenly last night that I thought I did something wrong."

Dana could hear the nervous laughter in Julia's voice, and she decided to lighten up the mood. Dana tried to make up an excuse, but Julia could read her pretty well.

"I was just tired, that's all," Dana tried to explain to the older woman, but she was not having it.

"Okay dear, we'll do all the shopping and we'll be there in an hour."

Since Dana came to work for them, they took to her right away. They even started protecting her like she was their own daughter, after the ordeal she went through with that monster she married. Julia winced as she thought about him with disgust. She would make sure Dana would never go through an ordeal like that again.

She noticed the instant attraction between Vernon and Dana; she had brought him here to watch over her, so to speak. The thought of Dana having someone near to protect her if needed pleased Julia and made her hopeful that this would be the start of something good for the both of them. She knew Dana would be angry with her if she ever found out Julia's true intentions, but what Dana did not know was the rogue of a man had been inquiring about her and her whereabouts. He was sending people in the restaurant asking all sorts of questions about her, one of them was a private investigator. No one gave any of them any information but knew it would only be a matter of time before he found out everything he wanted to know.

She knew if Dana found this out, she would be a nervous wreck, and that's why they hired Vernon. Of course, he would help her out with openings and fill in for her when it came time to travel so she wouldn't have to leave Eric; he would be there whenever she needed him to be. He was a man that was fully capable of taking care of things if they got out of hand. She knew this because she and her husband had done some investigative work on their own after they had met him. They found out Vernon Cruze could definitely take care of things if they did indeed got out of hand.

John and Julia arrived looking like they had gone grocery shopping for a month. They both kissed her on the cheek and then Eric; they loved her son and she liked watching them together. The phone rang in all the commotion and Eric told them that he would get it. John went to start the grill while Julia rambled on about a lady at the grocery store. Dana listened as she went on and on about the rudeness of this woman cutting her off at the checkout counter.

"Honestly sweetie, I don't know what's gotten

into people these days. No one has manners anymore and they definitely don't have any respect for older people. My parents would have skinned me alive if they ever heard that I acted like an animal out of their presence."

They were finishing putting away everything when Eric came in excited. "Mom that was grandpa, he wants to take me fishing right now. He said we will not be back until the morning. Can I go mom, please can I go?"

"Well what about Uncle John and Aunt Julia? They came all this way to see you, and you don't want to disappoint them, do you?"

He looked at Julia with a look of defeat then responded, "No."

Seeing the look on his face Julia interrupted, "Oh! Dana let the boy go! We'll have plenty of time to catch up. John and I are here for another two weeks and we'll find all kinds of fun things to do, won't we Eric?"

She winked at him like they had a secret code and his frown became a laugh of excitement again. Dana looked at them both, agreed, and told her son to go and get ready.

After seeing Eric off with his grandfather, Julia and Dana went back to the kitchen. Julia told her to relax and she started cutting up some fruit to go into the blender. "What are you making us?" she asked Julia. The woman smiled at her, remembering how she met her husband, so she told Dana the story of how they'd met and gotten married.

"Before John and I were married, I use to

bartend at some of the restaurants in Georgia."
Dana looked at Julia with surprise.

"Yes, I did. In fact, I was so good at it people use to request me for parties and such, I made good money. I made such good money doing it that I went to school for business management. John was one my clients. He and a couple of his friends threw a big party for his birthday and they wanted to keep track of the liquor supply. A mutual friend told him about me. At the time, he was the assistant manager for one of the hotels there. He reserved the V.F.W. to accommodate his guests and believe me, there were a lot of them. Needless to say, I made more money there than I had made at previous places. That's when our business partnership started among a lot of other things, dating being one of them."

Dana liked hearing her tell the story. It was amazing how you could be around someone and never really know them. It was also nice to hear that someone could find love and it lasted for an eternity.

"So, when did you decide to go into the restaurant business?" Dana asked her.

"Well, about ten years ago we were trying to think of a lucrative business to run. One that we could run ourselves with the experience we had and the thought of a diner that served alcohol appealed to us. You don't find any diners that serve alcohol, so we started a small mom and pop place. From there it took off and we went bigger and then you came along and helped make it even bigger. And for that we feel we owe you a lot, we love you, and will do anything for you."

Julia handed her a drink and sat at the breakfast nook beside her. Dana had not had a drink since she left Georgia behind, so when she took the drink from Julia, she felt like she was celebrating the beginning of a new life and that excited her. Dana took a sip of her drink and instantly liked the taste of it, nice and fruity but it still had quite a kick to it. Dana was happy with the way the day turned out. She was glad that John and Julia came by. It is what she needed; a grown-up day with plenty of sunshine, food and drinks with great company. She smiled as she looked at her friend who turned out to be a part of her family too.

"Father thank you for new beginnings. Thank you for giving me freedom to breathe again and surrounding me with good and loving people. Amen"

Not wanting her to feel cornered, Julia touched Dana on the arm. "Look, I know you don't like the idea of us bringing Vernon to help you, but we did it for your own good. Please be nice to him and you'll see in time that he's not bad at all, he's really a good guy and a wonderful person if you would just give him a chance. It is only business."

Dana looked at Julia surprised that she had even brought him up. She was even more surprised that she took up for him and recommended she give him a change.

CHAPTER SEVENTEEN

John came back in drying off his body. The water was wonderful, nice and warm just perfect for a day like this. "Where is my drink and what did I miss ladies?" he asked them as he walked up to his wife and planted a kiss on her cheek.

Julia looked into her husband's eyes as if it was the first time, she saw him. The doorbell rang as they gazed at one another.

"I'll get that so you can finish your drinks," John told them as he headed for the door. A few minutes later Vernon entered her kitchen with John, Dana took another sip of her drink while she eyed Julia with a questioning look on her face. Julia jumped off the bar stool and went to greet him. Dana eyed him up and down and was taken aback at how good this man really looked even with jeans on. She took in every square inch of his physique and did not hear him when he spoke to her. She noticed how the kitchen got unusually quiet and when she looked up and saw everyone looking at her, she winced. Then she saw Julia smirking at the reaction she had when he first came in.

"Hello," Dana spoke to the man standing in front of her smelling like he had taken a bath in heaven, then she looked away as if he burned her. Julia started chattering away, but she didn't know what the woman was talking about, because of the awareness of the man standing in front of her. By the time she looked up, Julia had went to fix more drinks. Dana was well aware of the man in her kitchen and he was aware of her too. He decided to break the ice and call it a truce.

"You have a beautiful house," he told her. "You chose a very beautiful community. Every home on this street is just as beautiful, I know the property rate is phenomenal. Oh, and I'd like to meet this son that I keep hearing about, I hear he is an intelligent one."

Dana was surprised that he knew about Eric and that he asked about him.

"He's out for the day with his granddad," Dana felt like an idiot. How could she let the mere sight of this man have an effect on her like this? She snapped back to reality and regained her focus. They all sat and talked, John telling stories about when he and Julia were younger, Vernon revealing a little about himself. She had started relaxing and was actually enjoying herself and thanking Julia for making the wonderful drinks.

After about two hours of chatting, Julia asked, "Is everybody ready to eat?"

"What are we having?" Dana asked eyeing John.

He answered, "Let's ask our chef," and they all looked at Vernon and smiled. Dana was surprised. She'd never let a stranger cook for her before, especially not in her own kitchen. She didn't know what to say and she definitely did not trust a stranger going through her things.

Everyone was watching her now and she had the weirdest look on her face as she looked back at them. At a loss for words, she stood there pondering what to do next and wondering what was about to happen.

It was Julia who spoke first. "We did not think you would mind dear, after all, who can say that one of the finest chefs came to their home and cooked them lunch personally?"

Dana hesitated at first, but then came around. It was only lunch and he was cooking for all of them, not just her. She nodded her head in agreement and took another sip of her drink. If she was going to get through this day, with a strange man in her house going through everything in her kitchen like it was his own, she would need more of Julia's concoctions to get her in the swing of things.

Vernon moved around her kitchen with ease, finding everything he needed without her help. She decided that she would rearrange her kitchen when they all left. She snickered to herself, she knew she was being petty, but so was John and Julia bringing him here without warning. But she loved them anyway like her own family, so she would endure for the day.

Everything smelled terrific. She watched as he used only the freshest of items and the combinations of spices and herbs blended in nicely, making her kitchen smell like a five-star restaurant. She couldn't help but notice that Julia and John waited until the coast was clear, then left them in the kitchen while they took a dip in the pool.

Vernon would not let her help him with anything but refilling his glass with the drink Julia had made for them earlier, *and what a drink it is,* he thought. They talked about his life and how he got started in the catering business. Dana listened as he told her about his marriage, his divorce and his kids; he was a very interesting person and quite humorous. He asked her about herself and Eric, being mindful not to bring up what he already knew. He listened as she talked, noticing how her eyes would light up whenever she talked about her son and when she smiled her face looked like a ray of sunshine. Once she felt relaxed and comfortable, she was nice to be around. They talked until he finished cooking. They laughed and joked about different recipes and she even tried to trick him a few times for a sample or two.

John and Julia came back in right at the time he was finishing up. He plated everything and it looked great. He was definitely a true culinary artist! Dana helped Vernon take the food out on the patio, her mouthwatering from the aromas coming from the dishes he prepared. John and his wife grabbed the plates and the wine glasses out of the cabinet along with a bottle of chilled wine and followed them outside.

Dana realized they forgot the silverware and turned to go back in and get some, but Vernon, reading her mind, stopped her then wink and told her to relax and have a seat, he would go back in to get some. John and Julia noticed the exchange between them and was pleased with what they saw. They were all admiring the dishes he prepared when he returned to the patio. John complimented him on the presentations of both dishes. Dana was excited, she was in the kitchen with him when he started and now there were two beautiful dishes sitting in front of her that made her want to devour them just looking at them.

He made grilled sea scallops with green onion relish and warm bacon vinaigrette and grilled spice rubbed shrimp nicoise salad. She eyed both dishes then looked at Vernon with appreciation in her eyes; he smiled and nodded his head then sat down beside her. John and Julia noticed again the exchange in looks, eyed one another and smiled. This was getting better by the minute. Lunch was served.

They talked, laughed and had a good time. The other couple was happy to see Dana let her hair down and enjoy herself finally. She had been through a horrible ordeal in the past and seeing her like this pleased them immensely. They secretly nodded a thanks to Vernon for helping them do it.

After they ate, everyone decided that it was time for the pool. Dana excused herself so that she could change; she showed Vernon to the guest room and told him that she would meet them outside. While Dana was changing, she thought about the day's events and how well it all turned out. She thought about her friends downstairs and Vernon. He was a very likable person and fun to be around, not to mention he could cook his butt off. Dana felt convinced that their working relationship would be a prosperous one and this made her feel more confident with him and the changes that were made.

Dana came out to the pool and Vernon thought he had died and gone to heaven from sheer excitement. She was a knockout! She had on a black and white bikini and curves in all the right places. She looked so good he had to whistle.

She glanced over at him and smiled, "No flirting by the pool please." Then she got into the pool.

He could feel his manhood waking up and he dove into the pool feeling like an adolescent. He thanked God for large swim trunks. They stayed in the pool for about an hour, before they decided to get out. Vernon was doing everything he could to keep his mind off of the gorgeous caramel woman drying off with her towel. Julia was rushing to make herself another drink and Vernon ran behind her saying, "Fix one for me too!" They looked at each other and laughed, then it grew silent. Dana saw him eyeing her up and down, taking in every curve and this made her shiver, sending goose bumps all over her body. She wondered what it would be like being held by him. She felt her eyes taking in every sculptured muscle until she came to his trunks. When she saw the outline of his member touching his thighs her eyes grew wide with surprise. She could hardly breathe, and this made her entire body shiver, so she turned and walked away from him and into the house.

Vernon cursed himself. The last thing he wanted to do was make her clam up again. He sucked his teeth and went into the house. Dana paced back and forth in her bedroom chiding herself. *Why did I wear this stupid bathing suit?* She took it off and threw it on the floor, drying herself with the towel. She thought about how he looked at her, how her body shivered when she looked at him. When she saw the muscle protruding from his body, she could not believe the size of him. The flames that went through her body.

She kept pacing back and forth until she turned and looked at herself in the mirror, "Get yourself together, you don't want this. Remember the promise," she reminded herself. She put her clothes on and went back down stairs. They were having drinks on the patio and when she took a seat, Vernon handed her one looking a little concerned. She took the drink and thanked him.

They talked about doing this again, seeing that it turned out to be a fun filled and relaxing day. Since they came down once a month, this would be a good way to let their hair down, especially with the planning and building of the other stores. They all agreed and clinked their glasses together in a toast. The women were so engrossed in conversation that they did not notice the men slip away. Dana thanked Julia for a wonderful day. She had not had this much fun in a long time, even if she was tricked into doing it. Dana and Julia were talking and laughing when the men came out onto the patio where they were sitting.

"Everything is cleaned and put away," John told them, he then patted Vernon on the back as they praised themselves on a job well done.

"Well hon, it's off to the condo we go, and maybe if you're good I'll give you a special treat," Julia told her husband.

Dana blushed when she heard the terms of endearment exchanged from the older couple. Vernon stayed behind for a while longer until she approved that all was well in her kitchen and the patio. He thanked her for the unforgettable day they had.

"I look forward to a lot more of these days," he smiled at her. "At work and off, I wasn't sure how well we would fit together, but I'm confident we will be great," he said with a smile.

It grew silent, then all of a sudden when she looked up at him, he grabbed her gently and kissed her long and slow. Dana felt her knees buckle. It felt as if all of the blood left her body and volcanically exploded between her legs. She leaned into him feeling the warmth of his body invade all of her senses; he stepped back from her, his breathing very heavy and she stood in front of him with every limb of her body shaking. He wanted to kiss her again but thought better of it. Then he turned and walked out of the door, leaving her standing there trying to catch her breath and wishing she would have stripped down to nothing and let him have his way with her.

CHAPTER EIGHTEEN

Knowing what she went through in the past, Vernon would not ask that of her or even expect that of her. In fact, he cursed himself for taking it that far, but she stood in front of him looking so beautiful, so alive. Today had brought a glow within her and she had not had that look before. Vernon saw the twinkle in Dana's eyes and saw what he could have with her. A life full of possibilities, a life he did not see there before. He swore to himself again. He would keep his distance until he knew that she was ready. He would keep it about the business at hand. With everyone gone now, Dana locked the door and went up to bed. She had to sleep off the day's festivities.

Dana felt the warmth of his hands teasing her and caressing her body, finding places she did not know she even had. Feeling the warmth of his breath on her skin as he kissed, licked, and teased one of her breasts then the other. The response of her body arching up to his as he tortured her with his teasing making her want more and more. He said her name in a low whisper with such passion as he entered her. Dana never imagined a feeling like this before. Her body squirmed under his, succumbing to every touch and every kiss, to his tantalizing words in her ear, drenched in sweat from the way he made love to her, then he told her he loved her.

Dana was awakened by the sound of a car alarm outside. She noticed she was breathing heavy and her body was trembled from the dream she just had of Vernon. It was so vivid, so real she could still feel him.

She got out of bed and changed her nightgown because the one she had taken off was soaked in sweat. She cursed herself and knew she had to get herself together if she was going to be working with this man. Trying hard to keep her mind off the dream was going to be hard, but she had to keep it professional because nothing other than that was optional. He was a man and they could not be trusted. She could not trust him with her heart or her life and with that she got back in the bed and went to sleep, not knowing that someone was lurking outside of her house in the middle of the night.

A week had passed since the gathering at Dana's house. John and Julia had gone ahead to Tampa. Vernon was to meet up with them when he arrived. He noticed how formal Dana was being with him, how she kept it business only. No joking around, no conversation at all unless it was about business.

Vernon suggested drinks after work one day and she refused him, saying that she thought it would be better if they kept everything on a professional level and she would appreciate it if he did the same. Her demeanor was cool and straight forward, but he knew that she felt something that night when he kissed her. He could feel it in the way she responded to him and lust had nothing to do with it. But he would respect her and her wishes. This was different. He thought he knew women from his dealings with them in the past, but this one was the one he always wanted but could never find. He was not one to believe in love at first sight, but since the first time he had laid eyes on her he could not think of anything else but her. He would show her how a real man loves by showing her what a real man is. She focused on the restaurant and making sure it ran smoothly, she had a knack of dealing with people and that was what made her successful.

He was leaving for Tampa in the morning and would not see her for about a week if things went according to plan. But first, he had to see her and talk to her. He wanted to be around her although they had not spent much time together, Vernon knew that this was the woman God made for him. He could not explain it. His hand went to his head and he began to scratch it smiling to himself, *how could I feel like this about a woman I barely even know? Who, by the way, acted as if I am the last thing she'd be seen alive with*? Then he got an idea! About an hour had passed when her boss Julia called telling her all the things she needed from her. She suggested that she and Vernon have a meeting to brief him on what his part was before making the trip. Dana, not liking the idea of her and Vernon being alone together, agreed to it anyway. After all she was the boss. She had just finished talking to one of her managers when Vernon came into her

148

office. She looked up at him as he shut the door.

"Just the man I wanted to see," she said as she leaned back in her chair. "We need to go over some things before you head out tomorrow," she told him.

He smiled at her and nodded. "Good I was just heading out. How about we do it over drinks?"

Dana eyed him suspiciously, but he looked at her like he did not know why. "That's fine, I'll follow you. Where are we going?"

He looked at her then told her, "No, I'll follow you home so you can park your car. Then I'll drive. I would not want you to drink and drive. I'll feel better knowing that you made it home safely. I found a nice little place at the beach that I think you'll like, so relax and let me do all the work." He winked at her as he noticed her reaction to that phrase.

Before she could refuse him, he made a promise that he would have her home at a reasonable time. Dana hesitated at first, but then agreed. They drove to a bar next to the beach where the lighting was dim, but cozy and the atmosphere was laid back, but very nice. They were taken to a table that was somewhat secluded and away from the bar and all of the goings on there, that way they would not be interrupted by the noise from the younger crowd. Dana ordered Riesling and Vernon a rum and coke. They talked about his trip and what was to be expected and even though he knew what was expected of him, he nodded and asked questions anyway just so he could hear her talk.

He ordered appetizers for them and Dana

ordered another glass of wine. He noticed how she started to relax as they talked. He would sneak in a few jokes here and there and every time she smiled the dimple in her face would deepen.

Dana asked him questions about himself and he answered each one, not holding anything back. He told her how he started cooking. What made him choose cooking as a profession and his idea to open his own business in the near future. He talked about his children and family, his past, his likes and dislikes. Dana listened to everything he talked about. She could see when something was sentimental to him, she could see when it was humorous. She could see in his eyes the love he had for his family and the work he did. The more he talked the more interesting he got. It was refreshing to her to have a conversation with a man that knew what he wanted and was taking the necessary steps to get there.

Dana was on her third glass of wine and it was now her turn. She talked about her son Eric and the relationship they had. She told him how he did not always live with her and talked about her past relationship in detail.

It was the first time she talked about it with anyone. She did not think she could, but now talking to Vernon, it all came out so easily and she was not affected by it one way or the other. She did not know if it was the wine, but she felt great. She thought it would be hard to talk about and there were times when she could not, but not tonight. What she thought would haunt her for the rest of her life did not.

She had gotten so engrossed in telling her story that she did not notice his hand over hers and when she gazed into his eyes, she could see something in them that was not there before. When she asked him if he was alright, he just nodded at her, called the waiter over to the table, ordered them another drink and asked for the check. He then changed the subject.

By the time they left the bar, both of them were feeling more than a little buzzed, so they decided to go across the street and take a walk on the beach. It was a beautiful night. The moon was bright, and the ocean air was just what the doctor ordered. They continued to talk about everything under the sun from childhood to music to movies. They laughed and walked until they noticed that they had walked so far, they had to turn around and walk back in the direction in which they came.

While walking back, Dana bent down to pick up a sea shell lying in the sand. He was watching her, and she had not noticed that he stopped talking until he took her hand in his, turning her to face him then he kissed her. It was a soft kiss, but a sensual one and she let him. The kiss lasted for what seemed like ages and when they came up for air, they were both trembling. He put his arms around her and held her and she did the same. Then they kissed again and walked to the car with his arm around her.

Dana's mind was twirling from the drinks and the salt air. This was a great night, but things were moving a little too fast. As they got to the car, Vernon let her go to open the door. Dana looked up at him then smiled. She stepped aside then got into the car. She watched him as he started the car then spoke. "I think we should keep things professional. I think we're moving too fast and I am not ready for this," she shrugged. "Most of all, I don't even know what this is. I'm not ready to share my life, my son or my career."

He looked at her thoughtfully before responding, knowing that it was fear speaking and not her heart. He could see it in her eyes and body language. So, he answered her. "I understand and respect your feelings and I will slow down, but I know what I feel, and I will prove it to you until I convince you that you and Eric will be the most important people in my life. And though I agree this is moving fast, even for me, the moment I saw you it hit me like a ton of bricks, and I don't want to shake that feeling off."

He paused for a moment then continued. "I will wait until you're ready, but I won't stop proving myself and I won't stop kissing you."

Dana felt flustered and at a loss for words. She was quiet for the rest of the ride. She closed her eyes and prayed.

"Father keep me from making the same mistake twice. I need to focus on my new life with my son. I need to focus on loving me and the next man that I get involved with will do all and be all that I want and need him to be. Amen."

152

CHAPTER NINETEEN

Neither of them spoke to the other, they only exchanged the occasional glance. Dana thought of the dream she had about Vernon, about the promise she made to herself long ago, but now something was changing in her. She knew she had to keep it together and that she would be alright. Nothing could take that away.

He pulled up in front of her house, got out of the car, and opened the car door for her. He then walked her to the front door. *And they say chivalry is dead,* she thought to herself. He put his finger under her chin to lift it up to his and he kissed her again, this time his lips felt lighter than a feather. He waited for her to unlock her door and go inside and when she turned to look at him, he leaned forward and kissed her one last time before he said goodnight. Dana was tempted to ask him to come in and she was disappointed when he did not suggest it on his own. This made her all the more interested in the man who had broken down the barrier that she promised herself she would not ever let down for anyone. She then locked her door and went upstairs to bed.

Vernon noticed a car parked a couple of houses down as he drove off down the street. It looked like the same car he saw when he left her house the night all of them were there. Both times there was someone sitting in the driver's seat. This seemed unusual to him especially in this part of town, so he decided to double back around to Dana's house. As he approached the street, he saw a figure getting out of the car, but when they saw the headlights of the approaching car they quickly got back into their car and took off.

This concerned Vernon even more, so he parked his car in her driveway turned, off the ignition, and decided to do a quick search outside of her house just to be on the safe side. When he saw that everything was okay, he decided to pay Dana another visit.

Dana had just changed into her nightgown when she heard the doorbell. Her heart raced as she thought about her night with Vernon. *Had he come back to finish what he started?* Curious, she put on her robe and went downstairs to answer the door, but before she reached the door the bell rang again. She looked out of the peephole and saw that it was him. He had come back after all. She opened the door in nervousness of what would come next.

His face was filled with tension as she moved to the side for him to enter. He did not say anything at first, he looked preoccupied then he apologized for disturbing her. He then told her what happened. "My tire went flat before I could get off the block good and I don't have a spare in my trunk as of yet. Would it be okay if I crash on the couch for the night? I promise to be a good boy," he said jokingly, but all the while feeling as though something bad was on the brink of happening. He felt like a rogue for lying to her, but he didn't want to upset her by his recent findings. Seeing that she had no idea he knew anything about her past but what she told him.

Feeling a little disappointed that he was not there for her, she nodded then answered, "Yes that would be fine, but I do have a guest room if you would be more comfortable there." Vernon eyed her up and down appreciatively, noticing the night gown that adorned her finely shaped body before declining her offer.

"No, the couch will be fine, but you can keep me company for a little while if that's okay with you," he smiled.

Her heart fluttered as she thought of them kissing earlier, how he teased her bottom lip in between his.

He could almost read her thoughts while watching her because he too could not stop thinking about her soft lips when he kissed her.

"A penny for your thoughts?" he asked her. She had been so enthralled in her thoughts that she did not hear him, so he walked up to her and kissed her just because, then he stepped back from her and asked her again, "A penny for your thoughts?" They looked at each other before she stepped back from him and told him goodnight.

Vernon walked around the house to make sure everything was secured before going into the living room. He saw the bar as he passed by and poured himself a nightcap before heading to the couch. His thoughts were on the car he had seen not once but on several occasions. He admitted to himself that it could have been anyone, but he wanted to feel safe in knowing that Dana was alright. He thought about the things she told him about her past, what she had been through. He had already been told by John and Julia, but to hear it from her was something different. The look in her eyes, her body movements, it was like she relived it all again, but then there was a release all at the same time. It sickened him even more to see her like that. She had gone through hell and back and gotten out alive. The idea of that left a sour taste in his mouth because not everyone made it out.

He wished he would have known her then. He would have made sure old boy would not walk again.

He thought about his ex-wife Shelly, and although they had been divorced for over a year when she got shot in the head by a guy she had been dealing with, she had been trying to leave him when it happened. Vernon and Shelly had three kids together and now they were motherless because some low life thought it was manly to scare her into staying with him instead of letting her go. His thoughts went back to Dana and since meeting her he could not imagine living life without her. He wanted to love her, and he wanted her to love him in return. He smiled to himself and shook his head. He never thought this would happen not like this anyway. He had finally met a woman who not only breathed life into his loins but his whole entire world and he would do whatever he had to do to make sure she was protected.

Dana tossed and turned just about all night. Knowing that Vernon was downstairs sleeping on her couch made her senses scramble. She had not felt like this before. Sure, she knew what it felt like to have feelings for someone, but not like this. This was different. He made her want more and that was a hard pill for her to swallow. She had sworn off men totally and now she could not stop thinking about this man who interrupted her world just with his presence.

It scared her because she did not know if she was ready or even wanted to give up the one thing that had been hurt so badly, her heart. The problem in this was that she thought she already had.

The next morning, Dana woke to the smell of bacon and coffee and the aroma was so delicious that she got out of bed, took a shower and went downstairs to see what Vernon was up to. He must have heard her coming because he was holding a mug of hot coffee out to her when she entered the kitchen. He had set the table with her best plates and in the middle, he had French toast, fresh strawberries, and bacon. He asked her how she liked her eggs over easy was her answer without looking at him because she was admiring the food he prepared.

"How long have you been up?" she asked him.

Watching her expression, he just smiled at her then he answered, "A couple of hours give or take. After barging in on you last night this is the least, I can do."

She smiled at him appreciatively. "Wow, thanks. A girl could get used to this you know," she said jokingly and for a moment their eyes connected and all of their thoughts of the kisses they had shared the night before surfaced.

"What time is your flight she asked him?"

He hesitated at first then he answered

"Well plans have changed. I talked to John and Julia and they told me that there was no need to come after all. They said things were going much better than they had expected and they did not need me. However, they did say they wanted us to take a couple of days off to relax and that they had already talked to Linda at the restaurant. We are not to go near it by any means."

Dana was surprised hearing all of this. Linda was the manager of the restaurant and anything she needed she had to go through Dana first, but she was fully capable of running it herself without anyone being there. Dana grew suspicious. She could not think of a reason as to why they would do that without talking to her first. Vernon must have read her thoughts because he chimed in saying, "I told them you were sleeping, and they did not want me to wake you. They said that you already worked too hard and that I was to make sure you did not go near the place." She nodded and continued to eat the food he cooked for her, enjoying each and every bite she took of it.

He changed the subject, "So, have you ever been fishing?"

Dana smiled at him before she answered, "I am a born fisherman, why do you ask?"

He nodded his head in surprise to her response because she was the only woman he knew that did not wince at the idea of it. "Okay then, we shall see. How about we take Eric with us? It's about time we spend some time together don't you think?"

It was Dana's turn to be surprised and surprised she was. Before agreeing with him, she hesitated for a brief moment. Vernon picked up on the immediate worry then stated. "Don't worry, I won't move too fast on him. We'll start off being good pals, how about that? Now go and get ready I'll clean-up," he told her and off she went. She had to pick Eric up from his grandparents' house, so she made the call and on their way they went. He took them to the Jetty's to fish. Nothing but a big wide ocean and oyster beds to boot and it was filled with a lot of other people fishing and lounging about. It was an awesome place and they had the time of their lives.

Eric was a little apprehensive at first, but then Vernon won him over when they made a bet about who could catch the most fish. It was a battle of wills, and she enjoyed every minute of it. It was a great day for fishing, and they were plentiful to say the least. Eric ended up catching four whiting, Vernon caught six catfish and Dana of course caught two reds, four catfish and two whiting which by the way made her the winner, so the men had to clean and cook the fish.

Vernon had an idea, so they made a couple of

stops before heading home. Dana could not remember the last time she had fun like this. She was so engrossed with work and spending time with her son that she forgot what it was like to go fishing or picnicking. She and Eric did other things like go to the movies or the game rooms and sometimes to the beach, but never fishing. Her son always went with his grandfather; he enjoyed it so much she did not want to take that time away from them.

Back at the house and now in the kitchen, Vernon started unloading bags. He poured Eric some apple juice and he and Dana a glass of wine, then he made a toast. "Here's to one of the best days of my life and it only gets better from here. How about we change into our swim clothes and take a dip in the pool?"

Eric was ecstatic as he jumped up and down, then Vernon broke in, "But first I must prep the fish for our fish fry." Eric was excited! He always enjoyed cooking the fish as well as catching them. This did something to Dana's heart. She had not seen him like this with anyone but his grandparents and John and Julia. She was happy that the two of them got along so well. It made her feel a little more optimistic about things and Vernon.

Vernon ordered everybody out of the kitchen while he cleaned and scaled the fish, telling them to go and get ready for the pool.

Both Eric and Dana did as he asked so that he could get things together and when Dana came back down to the kitchen, she heard her son and Vernon talking and laughing. She was in a good mood, so she could not wait to join in.

When she entered, Vernon whistled at her. She giggled then he winked at her. "Where have you been all of my life?" he asked her.

She giggled some more then replied, "Hiding from you."

He smiled at her, "Oh really, I have seen your kind before," they both laughed.

"I doubt that you have Sir, because if you had, we would not be having this conversation, now would we?"

Noticing that they had an audience, Vernon nodded his head then he replied, "Touché."

The phone rang and Eric ran to answer it. Vernon never got enough of looking at her and seeing her smile. "How about another glass of wine?" Vernon asked as he poured her and then himself some.

They talked as he cleaned the area he had been cleaning the fish on when Eric ran into the kitchen.

"Mom that was granddad. He has tickets for us to see the movie Transformers and he said we're going for pizza afterwards, is it okay? I'll also be staying over tonight because grandma said she needs a strong boy like me to make sure granddad locks all of the doors before going to bed, you know how forgetful he is, and he needs me there to remind him what to do."

"But you have only been home a couple of hours and I thought you wanted to have a fish fry and swim in the pool."

He looked at his mother and Vernon with puppy

dog eyes and her heart melted. He knew she had a hard time telling him no, and this was to be their day with Vernon. She was so looking forward to them all spending time together.

Dana started to tell him he could not, but she knew he wanted to see that movie. She had promised him that he could go see it with his granddad and she did not want to break that promise.

He came over to where she was and kissed her cheek. "Please, please, please mom?"

Dana saw the look in his eyes as he waited for her to give him the go ahead. She hesitated at first, but then gave in to him, he had been talking about that movie since he saw the previews and she did not want to disappoint him.

Vernon watched as the pair came to an agreement. He liked the relationship the two of them had. It made him think of the relationship he had with his own mother. She was his best friend and it was because of her he had such respect for women. In general, she had a tough life, but she never gave up and she taught him to do the same. He looked at the two of them again, then he commented, "I guess it's just you and me kid," then he winked at her.

Eric responded with wide eyes. "Yes mom, you have Vernon here with you, you won't be lonely."

Dana smiled at him and told him to go and get ready. He started to run, but then turned back around. "Oh! Don't forget to save me some fish please." Then he ran off.

"You bet buddy," Vernon answered him, then he too excused himself to go and change. While he was in the guest bedroom changing, he thought about how well the day went, thinking that Eric would be a bit shy at first and very protective of his mother. Vernon was actually pleased at how well the two of them got along. So well. In fact, he was sorry to see him leave. He wanted to suggest that they all go to the movies but thought against it. It was evident that he wanted to go with his granddad, and he did not want to move too fast. He wanted Eric to be comfortable with him and around him. Besides, with all that happened the night before, Vernon thought it to be wiser that Eric stayed at his grandparents'. He thought about the noise that had awakened him at five in the morning. When he went outside to look around, he saw a knife sticking out of Dana's back tire with a note attached saying, *"I am going to kill you whore."*

Vernon was so angry when he read the note, he snatched the knife out of the tire, looked up and down the street to see if he saw anything out of the ordinary, but no one was out there but him, so he went back into the house, folding the note and putting it in his pocket. He called John and Julia to tell them everything and that's why they told her to take a few days off. He did not want to freak her out about what he had found, so he took the tire off her car and went to buy a new one. By the time she had awakened, he had gone to the police station to give them a heads up on what was going on. He had friends there. He knew they would work with him and not involve Dana unless they had no choice in the matter. He came back, put the tire on her car and started cooking breakfast. He did not tell her anything and that's the way he wanted to keep it until he found out if this was some kind of sick joke or if she was truly in real danger. Feeling disgusted, he put his head down and thought of a time that changed the lives of he and his children.

"I promise on everything true, when I come face to face with this deranged woman abusing psychopath, he's going to wish to God he never existed. No one will ever hurt Dana again. EVER!"

CHAPTER TWENTY

When he returned downstairs, Dana was hanging up the phone. She had a puzzled look on her face that he could not read.

"Bad news?" he asked her.

She looked over at him nodding her head. "No, that was Julia. She said everything was going well, but then she went on about how worried she was about me. It did not make any sense. I mean, why would she be worried about me?"

He walked over to her and put his hand on her shoulder. "I would not let it get to me. You know Julia. She and John probably had a couple of drinks and she started thinking of you, and you know how protective she is of you and Eric."

Dana listened to him as if she agreed, but something in her spirit just did not feel right, so she would pray about this just like she prayed about everything else.

Vernon went and poured her glass of wine and handed it to her, then he did the same for himself. He then went to the cupboards and pulled out the pot he needed, smiled at her, and asked "Now, who wants fish?"

She watched as he moved around the kitchen with ease. It reminded her of the first time he cooked in her kitchen. It was like he belonged there. He had no trouble finding everything. It was almost as if he placed everything in its spot himself.

Dana thought about how comfortable she had become with Vernon. Though when they were at work she never wanted to mix business with pleasure, the more she did the more he invaded her thoughts, her dreams and her beliefs.

Dana's thoughts went back to a time when love hurt her physically, emotionally and verbally. A time when everything about her life was a lie, especially the man who was in it. It seemed long ago; three years in fact. It did not affect her now like it did back then, but every now and again she would cringe at her past and thank God that he brought her through it.

She was so lost in her thinking that she did not hear Vernon talking to her. It was only when he kissed her on the lips very gently that she snapped out of her thinking and kissed him back.

"I have the fish seasoned, the pot ready to go and the salad made. How about the pool? I could use that swim now," he said while looking her half naked body up and down in the orange show-it-all bikini she wore. The things he thought about doing to her at this moment were a damn shame. He looked into her eyes and shook his head. "You have me wrapped around your finger, I am yours and yours alone."

Dana looked surprised at his romantic declaration for her. Before she could respond, Vernon gave her a quick kiss on the lips and pulled her outdoors where the pool was.

The rest of the day went by with eating and lounging around the pool. Listening to the mellow sounds of the Isley Brothers, sipping on wine and having great conversation.

She had not experienced this much fun and laughter for as long as she could remember, and she loved every minute of it. She liked having him around because he gave her a different feeling, one that she could enjoy. She liked being with him, she liked the feeling that nothing was expected of her unless she desired it, but even at those times nothing happened. She was learning to appreciate him day by day because he showed her that it was not about sex. It was about companionship, friendship and partnership, and she needed that in her life, she depended on it. But was she ready?

Night fell upon them. When they noticed they'd drank three bottles of wine, they got up to clean the kitchen and take out the trash. Afterward, they sat down in the living room to watch a movie. Dana had started a collection before she came to Florida and she had a nice variety of them. They went through a few of them until they both agreed to a suspense drama.

It started off interesting and the plot was a good one. They sat on the sofa, his arm around her as her head rested on his chest. Neither of them realized just how tired they were, and they soon fell asleep in each other's arms. They slept for hours and it was Vernon who woke first still groggy from the wine. He looked down at her sleeping face, she was even more beautiful with her eyes closed. He bent his head and kissed one eyelid then the other. He got up from the sofa trying not to stir her, then he turned off the T.V. with the remote.

As he bent down and picked her up, she moved against him waking just a little. She looked up at him as he carried her up the stairs. He was still a little tipsy from the wine they had consumed earlier and all he needed to do was to sleep it off. He looked down at her and she laid her head on his shoulder as he walked down the hallway to the bedroom. He pulled back the covers with one hand as he supported her with the other and laid her down then pulled the covers back over her.

Vernon kissed her on the forehead and headed for the door, but before he got to the threshold, she called out to him still half sleep and a little tipsy.

"Vernon, would you stay with me tonight? I don't want to be alone."

He turned to look at her surprised that she asked him to stay the night. He blew out a long slow breath as if to get his mind right, not wanting their first time to be like this, but not wanting to disappoint her either. He walked over to the bed and got in beside her. Not wanting anything else to transpire, he laid on his back. She scooted over to him, laid her head on his chest and put her arm around him.

"I want you to hold me tonight," she told him.

He smiled to himself as he turned over and put his arm around her as she requested. She made a noise as the warmth of his body wrapped around her, then she drifted back to sleep.

He lay with her in his arms the entire night not letting her go once. When she turned, he turned and vice versa spooning off and on throughout the night. He tried not to wake her since he couldn't fall asleep right away. The smell of her skin was so intoxicating. Hell, everything about her was intoxicating. She was so beautiful, and he wanted to spend the rest of his life telling her so.

They both lay in bed. He in his swim trunks; and she had put a tee shirt over her swim suit. He could feel the softness of her legs on his, the warmth of her breath on his chest, and her heart beating against his. Vernon was captivated by this woman lying beside him, the last thing he remembered before drifting off to sleep was the faint smell of apples coming from her skin. They cuddled in each other's arms the rest of the night.

They slept as if they had been sleeping together for all of their lives, neither ever knowing peace like this before until now.

Morning came with the sun shining brightly through the window; Dana could hear the birds chirping. She had not felt this good in a while. As she lay in bed basking in the warmth of the body next to her sleeping so soundly. She stretched her limbs trying not to wake him and not wanting to move from the one thing that made her feel safe.

She ran her hand across his chest, exploring the hair that dwelled there. She proceeded to his stomach tracing the outline of his six pack. She took note at how his body would stiffen at her feather light touch from time to time.

She noticed that his breathing had changed from a slow, steady pace to a quickened one. She also noticed that he was now running his fingers down her back, rubbing ever so slowly. His touch was soft and sensual, and it sent heat waves pulsating through her whole body. She moaned. Her hand teasing him as it went further down his body until she reached his thick pulsating erection.
Dana could feel the blood racing through her body as she rubbed and fondled his swollen muscle.

Vernon let out a low moan. This woman had sent him over the deep end just by her touch. *Is this really happening to me,* he thought as his senses whirled out of control. With one swift move, he found himself on top of her looking into her eyes. Both of them out of breath from the sheer excitement of just being touched by the other; both wanting and longing for more.

He gazed into her eyes, wanting to make sure this is what she wanted and without having to ask her she replied "Yes."

He kissed her in a way that had her whole body shaking, making her arch up into his. He nibbled one ear then the other. Tracing his tongue down her neck kissing and teasing her, his breath was warm against her skin. The feel of his body on top of hers made her heart beat faster.

His manhood pressing against her had a dizzying effect on her that took her breath away. No man had ever made her feel this way. Her hands explored his back as she felt the firmness of him, traveling around to his chest, feeling every muscle.

He lifted his head to look into her eyes and then he kissed her on the lips and asked her, "Are you sure you're ready for this?"

Her eyes were hazy with want as she lifted her face to his and kissed him. Her tongue traced his lips then took his bottom lip between hers and sucked it very lightly. She had waited for a long time to feel this way and she had wanted this from the moment she saw him. She knew from the very first time their eyes met that she wanted him. She put her legs around him and pulled him closer to her. He kissed her again and knew once more that her answer was yes.

He made love to her slowly. Kissing and teasing her body in ways she had not experienced. He kissed and nibbled her neck and earlobes so softly that Dana thought she would go out of her mind with excitement. With his tongue, he traced her body stopping at her breast, tantalizing one then the other leaving nothing untouched until she called out his name. She moaned from the sheer pleasure of it all.

He got to her inner thighs kissing and tracing his tongue up and down, biting softly, then nibbling at them both. Taunting and teasing her watching her body shake and her eyes glaze over, he went to that most sensitive place that lay hidden between her legs. He kissed her then he licked and suckled her so softly and with such a hunger that it sent Dana into a multitude of spasms, her body and her mind out of control. Tears ran from her eyes as she received the deliciousness being given to her.

Dana's body shook violently, and she laid there trying to soothe her senses. Vernon rubbed and kissed Dana's body from head to toe. He wanted to give her every part of himself, not holding anything back. She was with him now and he would never miss an opportunity or day of showing her how much he loved her, wanted her, and needed her.

She reached up and pulled him towards her, turning him on his back. He had made her feel like nothing in this world mattered to him more than her and she believed him.

Dana climbed on top of Vernon while kissing and teasing his lips, his tongue, his neck, making her way down to his body exploring every crevice of him as she made her way to his chest. Hearing his heavy breathing, moaning and whispering of her name sent her to new heights.

With every touch of her hands, her tongue and her lips, this man was also in a world of his own. She continued until she reached the destination she had been seeking. She took him into her mouth and gave him the pleasure he had given her. When she thought he couldn't stand it any longer, she lay down beside him and held out her hand to him.

Vernon laid his body on top of hers and entered her with such gentleness. Dana thought she would lose her mind as she arched her body to meet his. He moved in such a precise rhythm that it took her breath away. He kissed her and whispered to her, his voice deep and sultry with every stroke. Sweat poured off of his body onto hers and she took every grind and thrust meeting it with her own. They continued their journey into raw ecstasy all morning bringing one another to explosive, mind-blowing climaxes over and over again. Losing themselves in their lovemaking and each other.

Afterwards, they lay in bed holding each other, both panting. She had finally met a man who when he kissed her there was no doubting in her heart and when he touched her, he touched her soul.

She never knew this much passion, this kind of connection, this type of communication between a man and a woman. When Vernon made love to her, he did so in every sense of the word. Heart, body, mind and soul. They fell asleep in each other's arms. Exhausted and satisfied.

CHAPTER TWENTY-ONE

It had been a wonderful six months. Work went on as usual and everything was going great. The other stores were up, running and doing well. There was a lot of hustle and bustle, but that was to be expected.

Dana and Vernon's relationship had taken off to new heights. He and Eric got along so well, in fact they were spending a lot of time together, so much that she missed out on a lot of cool things they did because of her work schedule.

One day they decided to make a picnic and take Eric to the beach. It was a beautiful day for it. Her favorite beach was Atlantic Beach because it wasn't as crowded. She liked that it had an adjoining picnic area where you could grill if you wanted to. She always preferred being closer to the water where she could see and smell the salt water air. Eric loved it and they would go twice a month during warm days. That was before Vernon came into their life. Now they went all the time.

Today was especially nice because they were all together and he and Eric made plans to play in the water all day. They also got a chance to play some volleyball with some of the locals there. They tried to get her to play but she opted on reading a book. It was by one of her favorite authors, T.L. Tucker.

She had a knack for capturing the essence of her characters and that made her books easy to love and read. Dana was looking forward to reading it.

Dana was engrossed in her book when they returned. Both of them out of breath announced how hungry they were. They dug into the chicken and potato salad they brought along with them.

Still reading, she could not help hearing the two of them laughing and joking when Eric asked, "Are you and mom going to get married?"

Dana's jaw dropped so wide she thought she would need super glue to put it back. She looked at her son in amazement still not knowing what to say. All the while Vernon had been looking at her response to that question. She glanced at him unaware that he had been watching her the whole time.

He smiled at her then asked, "Would that be such a bad idea?"

She looked at him, her eyes wide, her thoughts racing

"Why are you encouraging him?"

He had a sheepish grin on his face as if he was toying with her. He actually thought this was funny. Dana grew agitated at first but then she saw the puzzled look on Eric's face like he had missed something. He looked at her then at the man sitting next to him.

Vernon seeing how uncomfortable she was, changed the subject. "Last one in the water has to wash mommy's car for a month!"

Eric hearing this jumped off the bench and ran

to the water like his life depended on it.

Vernon still watching her face responded, "The thought had crossed my mind. I don't see anything wrong with him asking a question. Besides, can you honestly say that you haven't thought about it? I mean not now, but in the future. You know I am in love with you, so why hide the fact that I think about it?"

He saw Eric jumping up and down like he had just won a trophy. He got up from the table and then he was gone.

Dana sat there in silence; still stunned. *Did he say he was in love with me?* Her heart was racing. This was the last thing she expected to hear today.

Even if she did think about it, she knew that things would change between them and she did not want to risk that. Marriage was not for her and she knew it. She had always wanted to be married but when she did, it proved to be betraying, abusive and life threatening. No one should ever have to live like that. She was blessed to have gotten out when she did, because few women do. They end up dying because they never left. Nate had tried to kill her, and he almost succeeded. She thought,

"Thank you, God, for your perfect timing in all things. Thank you for my new life and thank you for peace of mind. Amen."

Dana was so deep in thought she did not see the strange car or the man behind the steering wheel parked at a distance, but Vernon did. He got Eric and they walked to where Dana was sitting. When the stranger in the car saw them heading towards her, he drove off.

Vernon, not wanting to alarm her, started packing up everything they brought along with them and said it was time to leave. She noticed the sudden change in him. He seemed to be distressed about something. The features in his face were tight and he was quiet on the drive back to her house.

She wondered, *did I offend him in some way?* She put her hand on his arm and asked him if he was okay. He looked over at her and shook his head. He tried to smile but it did not reach his eyes, so she left it alone.

Back at her house he unpacked the car and made sure they got in safely. He then turned to her with a stony look on his face "I have to take care of something. I'll be back shortly." Eric looked up at him and started to protest, but Vernon started first, "How about pizza for dinner?"

Eric was ecstatic now running upstairs to his room. Vernon took her face between his hands and kissed her lightly on the lips "I'll be back," he told her and then he left.

Puzzled at what was going on, she stopped at Eric's room. "Don't forget to shower," she told him. Then she went to her own her room to do the same. When she entered her room, she looked at her bed and remembered the times he had occupied it.

Dana and Eric were looking at movies when Vernon returned. The smell of pizza filled the room as he walked over to them and they were glad to see him because hunger had set in. They ate pizza and looked at movies for the night.

Eric fell asleep on the floor, he had a long day in the sun. Dana woke him and told him to go to bed. Half coherent, he got up, bid them goodnight and did as he was told.

The phone rang and Dana got up to answer it, but it was Vernon who said, "I have it." He picked up the phone. "Hello," he answered in a calm tone. The caller sneered then replied, "You failed once, you will fail again!"

Vernon hung up the phone and ran to the window. Just as he opened the curtains a car drove by. It was the same car he had been seeing outside of Dana's house and from the beach.

Dana watched his every move and grew concerned. "What's going on Vernon?"

He looked back at her and answered, "Nothing."

Dana was starting to get worried. "Who was that on the phone?"

Panic was in her face and he cursed to himself because she had witnessed this.

"A prank call, that's all. No need to worry," he told her as he walked towards her and put his arms around her. He noticed she was shaking, and he bent his head and kissed her on the mouth. She tried to push him away, but he would not let her go.

Dana could not help but feel like something was not right. She had felt this way for weeks. Now she knew that the feelings she was having were correct.

She pulled away from Vernon trying to keep her thoughts together. She went and poured herself a glass of wine. Vernon was behind her and followed suit. She stepped back from him

"Is it another woman?" she asked him.

Vernon almost choked on his drink as he looked at her with complete disbelief.

"Another woman! Why would you ask that? Don't you know how much I love you? How can you stand there and discredit me like that?"

The look on his face told Dana she should not have asked that question. "Well what is it? Why have you been so secretive lately? You have moments where you're hot one minute then cold the next. What's going on with you?" Vernon reached for her, but she backed up.

"Look, I'm a big girl and I already know the routine, so I'm going to make this easy for you. We need some time apart. Go do what you do."

"Dana! What are you saying?"

She looked at him and head held high. "I'm saying, leave my house, it's over!"

Stunned to say the least, Vernon could not believe how things were going. He tried desperately to explain himself but to no avail. She had turned a deaf ear to him.

"Leave now!"

She went to the door and opened it for him. Vernon hesitated at first, but when he saw the look on her face, he respected her wishes.

"Damn!" he cursed before walking out the door.

Dana closed the door and locked it. She walked

179

over to the window. Vernon was on his phone as he unlocked the doors to his car. He had a frustrated look on his face and Dana could see that he was in a heated conversation.

Tears streamed down her eyes and the feeling of defeat tugged at her heart. She had managed yet again to give her heart to a man who did not deserve her. She closed the curtains, turned out the lights and went up to bed.

CHAPTER TWENTY-TWO

"Rodney, I need you to run a tag on a black 2008 Chevy Lumina, tag no# ZYZ 008 Florida."

Rodney took down the information. "Man what is this about?" his friend asked.

"It's about Dana, she's being stalked, but she does not know it. While you're at it, can you run the name Nate Johnson for me?"

His friend wrote everything down.

"Also, I am going to need some more favors from you."

The other man listened as Vernon spoke then responded, "Okay what do you need me to do?"

Vernon backed the car out of the driveway and headed for Rodney's. Rodney and Vernon had been friends for a long time. Rodney served on the police force for ten years. He had seen Vernon through some tough times in his life. They were like brothers, and right now he needed his help more than ever.

"Man, are you kidding? Why haven't you told her the truth?" his friend asked him, worried now for his friend and his relationship with this woman. The two men sat at the table drinking beers.

"I did not want to say anything until I was sure. You don't understand, this woman has been through a lot in her past. The man she was with back in the day almost killed her and I could not let her go through that again. Not without knowing that I was right about the hunches I have been having lately." Listening to his friend and hearing the torment in his voice, the other man got up from the table and got them both another beer.

"You know man, I have not seen you this bent over anyone like this before. She must be the one."

Vernon looked at his friend, his hands going to his head. He had to get her to listen to him. She had to understand that this was all for her.

"I need you to help me stake out her house. Let me know if you see anything or anyone unusual and if you do follow his ass so we will know where he's staying at."

Rodney nodded to his friend, "Okay, I'm there. Anything I can do to help out a friend. I'll get right on the info you gave me, and I'll call you when I find something out."

The two men shook hands, "Oh! One more thing, I need your car for a day or two."

Vernon sat in the car going over the events that took place earlier. He thought about the phone call and the heated discussion between he and Dana. He was shaking his head trying to think of a way to get her to talk to him.

How could she think he was seeing someone else? He thought he had made it clear how he felt about her and Eric. He thought he had shown her in everything he did, but yet she doubted him; she doubted his love for her.

If only she would talk to him, answer her phone.

He had called her five times already. Frustrated with how things turned out tonight, he sat in his friend's car at the end of her street, watching and waiting for the mysterious car to show up, but it never did. Vernon blew out a long slow sigh. He was there all night. He never took his eyes off of her house and he never left his spot not. His mind was on the only thing that meant anything to him. His love for Dana and keeping her and Eric safe.

Nate was in his room pacing back and forth looking at the pictures he had pinned on the wall. Some of them with the eyes cut out of them and some of them with the neck slashed. His eyes were dark as lacquer.

"Whore you thought you got away! That I would never find you!" he spat out.

"You thought I would just let you leave me like that? I told you that I would kill you first. Just like I told that broad back in Atlanta right before I slashed her throat."

Nate thought about the moment before he took the other woman's life. How she pleaded with him and told him she loved him. "What's wrong with these females? What makes them think they have what you need? She knew I was married, and she didn't care. So, she had to go too. Hey thanks for bailing me out of jail, I did your husband a favor. Now this whore has another man in my house, laying with her and doing whatever he wants to do to her and while raising my son!" Sweat poured off of his forehead as he paced around the room faster and faster. He didn't feel the blood running down his legs as he swung the knife slicing his pants.

"You thought the police would keep me from you?" he said as he snatched one of the pictures from the wall and with the knife in his hand stabbed it over and over again! He was so enraged that his thoughts went back to the past where his innocence was taken. A life lost because she wanted to leave him. His adrenaline pumped furiously as he heard the gunshot and saw the lifeless body fall to the floor. Blood draining from her head, no breath coming from her body. He cocked his head to the side, only this time he saw Dana's face and her body lying in a pool of blood. Still back in the past and unaware of his present surroundings

"I told you the first-time whore, nobody leaves Nate unless I want them to leave, and even then, they'd be carried out in a body bag."

His thoughts went back to the trial and the cops that were on the case. They thought they had enough evidence to get him sentenced for life, but he beat the rap by only serving eight years. He remembered the look on the cops' face when they heard the sentence. He looked at them and winked before he was escorted to the back. He later was told that the woman he killed was the ex-wife of one of the cops that were on the case. They had gotten divorced a year before she was killed. The cop heard that she had been seeing some low life who was taking all of her money. Nate sneered as he thought about that time in his life twelve years ago, and he managed to meet another one and marry her.

"It served her right, females like that deserved to be punished. That's why that homewrecker in Atlanta was punished. She didn't know her place. That's why Dana will be punished," Nate said talking to himself again.

She had him arrested almost four years ago. And he was not going to spend another day locked up because of any female he thought, *married women who go out and sleep around do not deserve to live.*

He thought of all the times he made love to Dana and pictured her doing the same things with this man. The faces she made. The way she responded to his touch, his lips. He took another sip of brandy as he thought of her and his plan. He would make her pay for all that she had put him through for the past four years, only he would torture her first. He took another drink then another. Soon he was passed out on the bed with pictures of Dana slashed up beside him.

Dana woke the next morning feeling down and depressed. She reluctantly got out of bed so she could start her day. She thought about the night before. *Why did I throw Vernon out of the house? What was he trying to tell me?*

"Snap out of it!" she told herself as she headed to her bathroom to take a shower. Afterwards she decided to call the restaurant to check in on things, this would give her time to think of something other than Vernon. Dana was downstairs drinking a cup of coffee and wondering what she would do on a pretty day such as this one. She was not needed at the restaurant, so she had time on her hands to do what she wanted. With everything going successfully at work, she did all of her paper work at home. She only popped in at the restaurant twice a month to check up on things and attend staff meetings. She was not needed for anything unless it was an emergency.

As she drank her cup of coffee, scenes from the previous night replayed in her head and the thought of Vernon flooded her heart. Did she really think he was cheating on her? Who was he talking to on the phone? What was he keeping from her? *So many questions, so few answers,* she thought to herself.

She remembered how he reacted to her telling him to leave. She also thought about the hurt she felt telling him to do so.

She knew how it felt to be a prisoner where love was concerned. She also knew that she would never repeat that cycle again. Eric came downstairs, rubbing his eyes he kissed her on the cheek as she sipped her coffee.

"Mom, it's teachers planning day today and my project is due tomorrow. Can we go get the rest of my supplies so that granddad can finish helping me? I told him you would drop me at their house when we were done."

She looked at her son, then gently then replied, "Sure sweetie, how about we go to breakfast first?"

Eric smiled at his mom, "Can we go to IHOP for pancakes?"

She watched him as the excitement grew in his

face, "Yes we can, now go get ready."

She took her cup to the sink and rinsed it out before putting it in the dishwasher, promising herself that she would make the most of her day by keeping herself busy and not thinking of Vernon. *Well at least it sounds good,* she thought as she went upstairs to get ready.

While they were at the restaurant eating, Eric turned to her and asked, "Mom, why were you fussing at Vernon last night?"

Taken aback by the question Dana tried to make light of it. "Honey I was not fussing at Vernon, it just sounded like I was."

Eric eyed her suspiciously not buying her story. "Then why did you tell him to leave? Don't you like him anymore? Because I do. I was hoping he could be my dad if it's okay with you."

Dana's mouth dropped in shock. She quickly tried to compose herself, not sure what to say or do, so she changed the subject.

"Are you finished your breakfast? We need to pick up your supplies. We don't want to keep your grandfather waiting."

They went for his supplies and she took him over to his grandparents' house. On her way back home, Dana's thoughts went to Eric and the questions he had asked her. She knew they had gotten close and that her son adored him, but what she did not know was how much her son had grown attached to Vernon. So much so, that he wanted him to be a part of his life and to call him his dad. The fact of the matter was that even with the current events, she too had grown attached to Vernon. Actually, she had fallen in love with him and now he was gone. She had put him out of her house and her life because of his secrets. Her heart broke as the regret sank in. *What will I do now,* she thought as she drove, not seeing the vehicle a few cars behind her as she headed for her house.

Vernon had not left her side since the squabble, he had not been to sleep since he left her house and when she and Eric left the house, he followed her the whole time. He was tired from the lack of sleep, but he was determined not to leave her side, even if it meant following her everywhere she went. He knew he had to get her to talk to him. That was the only way he would be able to make her believe he loved her. He wanted to tell her the truth, but he needed a little more time. Time, he knew was growing short and he had to get to the bottom of the matter and soon.

Dana drove up into the driveway and parked the car. Her mind was still on Vernon and the argument they had the night before. Did she overreact or were her feelings warranted? She did not give him a chance to explain, she had been too much into her own feelings to care about what he wanted to say.

She was fishing for the door key on her keychain when she spotted a bag on her doorstep. She looked puzzled at first until she realized that in it was a dead bird and a soiled pad. She dropped the bag and screamed. Suddenly panic stricken, she then fumbled to unlock the door, but her keys would not cooperate with her. Tears streamed from her eyes and down her face uncontrollably and her body was shaking with a fear so great that she could not think straight.

She was still fumbling with her keys trying to get her door opened and did not hear nor see Vernon when he called out her name from behind her. He had heard her scream while sitting in the parked car a couple houses up. He immediately got out of the car and ran to her. He saw how shaken she was, and he reached out and put his arm out towards her until he had her body close to him.

Dana was so blinded by fear that she tried to fight him off as soon as he touched her until she realized it was him and no one else. She was shaking so badly that he took her keys from her, opened the door and literally carried her in, cradling her body into his. He shut the door behind them and carried her to the living room where he placed her on the couch.

"My God, I don't know what put her state, but please bring her back to me."

When he looked at her, he saw tears rolling down her face. He exhaled slowly before approaching her.

CHAPTER TWENTY-THREE

He tried talking to her, but she would not respond. He left her sitting in the living room briefly while he went and fixed her a drink. Whatever it was, it upset her pretty badly.

He fixed her a Brandy then decided to fix himself one too, hell seeing her like this had him a little shaken up as well. He took her the drink hoping it would help her calm down so he could get some answers from her. She took the glass from him and took a gulp. The warm liquid burned the back of her throat making her gasp a little, but it still was not enough to calm her.

Vernon watched her closely, waiting for her to say something, anything at this point. She finished her drink and held out her glass for another one. He took her glass from her and walked back to the bar. He decided not only to pour her another, but this time he took the whole carafe as well. He gave her the second glass, taking a gulp of his own. He waited for her patiently trying to find some sign of serenity in her face, but there was none that he could see. He sat with her for what seemed like hours in complete and total silence before she reached out to him and touched his face lightly. He blew out a sigh of relief then continued sipping his drink in silence, not wanting to rush her in anyway.

It was Dana who broke the silence first.

"He's here," she said in a low, broken voice.

Vernon gazed at her, then he moved closer to her and put his arms around her trying to comfort her with the warmth of his body and the sound of his voice. "Who's here baby? What happened?"

Dana started telling him everything that took place from the time she got out of the car until the time she saw the bag and the contents in it. Vernon listened to her story calmly, all the time his blood boiled hotter and hotter with everything she said. *How in the hell did he get past me?*

"How do you know it's him?" he asked her.

She took her head off his shoulder, took another sip of her drink and looked into his eyes. "Because he has done that to me before." His eyes went wide with shock.

"Dana, we have to call the police, they have to find this bastard before I do."

He took her by the hand and walked to the front door, he opened it and went outside with Dana in tow. Vernon searched the premises but found nothing.

Dana watched anxiously as he searched, but still there was nothing. Panic started to arise in Dana again. He had come back to retrieve the bag while they were in the house.

Vernon saw the color drain from her face, and he ran to her at such a swift pace that had her in his arm before she could hit the floor. He swore to himself then they went back into the house and he closed and locked the door behind them. It was broad daylight and this man came and went from this house without being seen twice in one day.

Vernon took her back to the living room and laid her on the couch. He then went through the house checking all of the windows and doors until he was convinced that everything was closed tight and secured, then he went back to check on her. She was sitting up on the couch looking towards the window. She turned her head towards him when she heard him enter the room.

"I'm sorry about last night," she told him. "How long have you known he was here?" she asked him. Realizing that Julia and John must of have told him about her. Knowing now that was why he was so secretive with her. She looked at him searching.

Not wanting to keep her in the dark any more than what he already had, but not wanting to upset her anymore either, he had to answer carefully. She watched him as he struggled with the question. His eyes looked as if he aged overnight.

"Only a little while. I was not sure at first and I did not want to freak you out. I wanted to make sure I was right before I said anything. I have a friend on the police force checking out a few things, I'll give him a call to see if he found out anything yet."

Dana nodded her head in acknowledgment, "I'm going to take a shower."

He kissed her on the forehead. "That's my girl," he told her trying to sound as calm as possible as she made her way upstairs.

Vernon picked up the phone and dialed his friend. Rodney answered and Vernon told him everything that had gone on. The two men talked and then Rodney dropped a bombshell on him.

"I have some news for you and you're not going to like it one bit." Vernon listened to his friend. "This Nate guy, you'll never believe this man, you know him. He has crossed our paths before man," he told him.

Vernon listened, then answered now curious. "Yeah, how so?" trying to figure out what the man on the other end was referring to.

"I hate to bring this up bro, but the guy who killed your ex Shelly, is the same guy Dana was married to."

Vernon almost dropped the phone. He stood there frozen as he listened to his friend. "But get this, this Nate Johnson is not who he says he is. His real name is Brian Nathan Jackson."

"I don't know what was going on with Dana and him, but his family was in on it keeping everything hush hush."

Vernon's eyes closed as memories of the past came flooding back to him. A life lost and his children without their mother. They had been divorced for over a year when she was killed. He was one of the cops that had been assigned to the case, his friend Rodney was the other one. It had been a dark time for his children. Every day he protected and served a city with his whole heart and when it came to him and his children, they failed to do the same. That's when he gave his badge up and everything that went along with it. An unjust legal system that ended in an unjust trial. He was still in his thoughts when Rodney called out his name, snapping him back to reality.

"So now you know what's going to happen when we get the police involved. Once they start investigating this, they are going to pick it all apart."

Rodney understood where Vernon was coming from. He thought, *the two arresting officers are the same two dealing with the same maniac now.*

Anger overtook Vernon and his thoughts kept traveling from the past to the present, then back to the woman he was now in love with.

What were the odds for this kind of situation to cross his path twice in a lifetime? This man had struck one time, taking away the mother of his children and with just a slap on the hand, receiving little to no punishment. Now he's back and threatening the life of the woman who Vernon would spend the rest of his life with if she let him. The difference this time was that this bastard would never succeed. Was this fate or some kind of sick joke? Rodney broke through the silence again.

"Man, you have to tell her everything, and whatever you do, don't leave her side, not even for one minute."

"I'll stake out the place and when he makes a move, so will I. We'll catch him, don't worry. This thing will be handled once and for all." The two hung up the phone.

He was still standing in the same spot when

Dana came back downstairs. He was in deep thought this time about how this situation began and how it would have to end. He looked at Dana when she entered the kitchen. *God she was beautiful,* he thought. He reached his hand out for her to take and she did, suddenly he felt uncertain about how she would handle what he was about to tell her.

He took her in his arms and kissed her like it would be the last time and when they came up for air, Dana gazed into his eyes knowing that he was about to tell her something that would shatter her whole world.

"I need you to sit down; there are somethings I have to tell you."

Dana listened to Vernon as he told her every sordid detail of his past and the new news he had just gotten from his friend Rodney.

She took in everything he had told her not interrupting until he was finished. Her eyes were wide in amazement and her heart was pumping so fast and so hard she thought she would pass out from the sheer shock of it all. How could all of this be happening? Was this all true? She had been married to a man that she did not know anything about, not even his real name.

The room grew silent as both of their minds and their memories drifted to the past. Both of them remembering a time where life was stolen from them, hers with Nate and him raising his children who no longer had their mother.

Dana got up from the kitchen table and went to the bar to fix herself a drink and did the same for

Vernon. He watched her but said nothing. She had a somber look on her face, and he wondered what she was thinking. He felt a bit unsure about how things would turn out between them now that she knew the truth, but he was determined to keep her and Eric safe and he would not let her give up on him without a fight.

She gave him his drink without a word. For a long while the room was so silent you could hear a pin drop. He could see that she was trying to make sense out of this whole ordeal and her body language was somewhat languid.

She looked over at him and then she spoke

"It's funny how the world is; you can be with someone, sleep with someone and never know who they really are. On the other hand, you can be with someone and sleep with someone and never know how you're worlds coincide with one another."

She shook her head not knowing what to believe or who to believe in anymore. This was like some strange dream that she could not wake up from. She sat across from a man who at one time in his life encountered the same man who had come close to taking her life from her. Was this fate or was this his way of avenging the woman who had been taken away from their children prematurely?

She felt like a pawn in a chess game. She wanted to believe him, but her heart would not let her. She tried to grasp onto something, anything that would make her reach out to him. He had plenty of opportunities to tell her the truth about him, about his life, but he chose not to until now.

She was supposed to believe it was pure coincidence that all of this was happening?

Tears welled up in her eyes as she thought about everything that they both had been through because of one man. If all of this would not have happened would he have told her anything about his past? Looking at him through blurred eyes and a heavy heart she came to the conclusion that no, he never considered telling her the truth until now.

Seeing how she struggled with her thoughts, Vernon saw the doubting and the disbelief transform in her. He grew nervous and agitated all at once. This man had interrupted their lives once before, he would not do it again. The fact of the matter was that he was in love with Dana and he could not lose her. His life depended on it, she meant everything to him.

"Baby, I need you to believe that I love you and I would never do anything to hurt you. I am just as stunned by all of this as you are. If Rodney would not have done what I asked him to do I would have been just as much in the dark as you were."

Feeling desperate now, he got up and walked around to where she sat and got on bended knees where he could face her.

Not looking into his eyes, she asked, "Vernon, how come you never told me about your past before now?"

She watched him closely now trying to search out some truth in him.

"I mean you told me all about your kids, but you never told me about everything else, like for instance you being a policeman."

Vernon rubbed his hand across his head trying to find a way to get through to her. "Look I was not trying to hide anything from you. I did not tell you because it's still hard for me to talk about. My kids went through a tough time back then. They had their mother stolen away from them and because of that I had to bury what I felt so that I could be there for them."

"Were we together when she was murdered?" No, we were divorced. Did I love her? Yes, I did. She was the mother of my children; and for the first time in my life I felt helpless trying to pick up the pieces of their broken life."

Tears filled his eyes as he spoke, and she understood the burden he carried in his heart all of these years.

"No one knew about my life, but the people involved in it at that time. I am sorry if you feel uncertain or betrayed in anyway, but you are the first to know even if it came out in an unexpected way. It is what it is, but I need you to know that I love you and I never want to hurt you in any way. I need you right now and I need you to know that this will never happen again."

Dana's heart sank. She wrapped her arms around him and held him tightly, never wanting to let him go and he in return thanked God for letting her do so.

"I love you," she whispered in his ear then she kissed him.

"Father help us get through this chaos.   We can't do this without you," she silently prayed as she teared up in the arms of Vernon.

CHAPTER TWENTY-FOUR

Rodney returned Vernon's car to Dana's house. He made sure the doors were locked and as he made his way to his own car, he spotted a couple of teenagers as they drove down her street joyriding.

He did not worry about giving back Vernon's keys because just like him he kept a spare set. He got into his car and drove around the block once before parking at the end of the street. He stayed parked all night watching out for anything that looked unusual. He wondered if his friend was doing okay. Vernon was like a brother to him and his kids called him Unc. He loved them as if they were his own. They still called him from time to time to checked on him. They had been through a lot since the passing of their mother and if anyone ever deserved to be happy it was Vernon. This was some crazy shit going on, and of all his years being a cop he had never seen anything like this. This was surely a first in his career.

Three hours passed and still no sight of anyone, but then just as he thought it was going to be a quiet night, he saw headlights coming from behind him. The car was going at such a slow speed Rodney knew that something was up. The car passed by him with tinted windows, so he could not make out the driver. The car was a different make and model from the one he had inquired about days ago. He took down the tag number once again. The car continued down the road, then slowed down in front of Dana's house. He sat up so he could see better. He waited to see if the driver would get out of the car. But he did not, he just drove off after a couple of minutes. Rodney started up his car and followed while he called the station to run the tag.

He drove slow trying not to be seen by the driver in front of him. He went all the way up Beach Blvd. until he came to the Best Western there. Rodney parked and watched the man as he got out of the car and walk inside the hotel. He waited for a moment, then he got out of his car to check out the other car. He looked through the car windows but saw nothing suspicious, his phone rang. It was the dispatcher calling him back.

"Hey Rodney, the vehicle you called in was reported stolen this morning what do think about that?"

"Have you apprehended the suspect?"

He looked around but saw no one. "No I haven't. I just saw it parked illegally here at the Best Western up here at the beach," he told the officer.

"Okay, I'll call beach police and let them handle it," they hung up.

Rodney went back to his car and got in; he dialed Vernon before he started the car. He did not see the passenger in the back seat.

"Hello," Vernon answered but all he heard was scuffling, gurgling then the line went dead.

"Hello, Rodney!   Hello!   Hello, answer me man!"

In a panic, Vernon dialed his friend again, but he did not pick up that time either or the next time after that.

He tried calling numerous times, but his friend never answered. He ran out of the house and looked up and down the street, but there was no sign of his friend anywhere.

He went back into the house and closed and locked the door. Dana met him in the hallway. He looked like someone punched the air out of him.

"What's happened?" she asked him, but no sound came out of his mouth, she asked again.

"Baby what happened?" this time in a nervous tone. He gazed at her with a perplexed look on his face.

"I think I just heard Rodney get murdered."

Dana went pale and she put her arms around him as she cried out loud. They stood in the hallway of the foyer holding one another for comfort and strength. Spent from today's events she looked up at him,

"Babe you have to call the police and tell them what you heard," she told him, and then she took his hand in hers and led him to a chair in the kitchen. He picked up the glass from off the table and consumed the rest of the golden-brown liquid that had been in it, and then he made the call. He spoke to one of his old friends on the force that transferred when Rodney did. He gave him a detailed description of everything he heard when Rodney had called him.

He also told them that he had called him back numerous times, but still got no answer. The officer on the other line told him Rodney had called in about half an hour ago, but he spoke to another officer and that he would speak to that officer immediately to find out the details of the call.

"I'll call you back after I finish talking to him. I'm on this ASAP," the cop told him then they said they're goodbyes and hung up the phone.

The two of them sat at the kitchen table in silence for what seemed to be ages. Both not knowing what to do or what to say but to wait patiently. An hour passed by before the phone rang, Vernon answered.

"Hello what did you find out?" he asked the man on the other end.

"Vernon, I have some bad news. Rodney was murdered tonight. He was found in his car with this throat slit from ear to ear. Apparently, he called earlier tonight to run tags and it turns out that the car was stolen. No one was apprehended and it was the beach side police that found him." Vernon remained quiet, listening.

"We have every available car on the lookout for this vehicle. Don't worry man we will catch him if he's out there, I promise you that. In the meantime, I'm going to need you to come down and give a statement; he also has you as his last living relative so you're going to have to identify the body."

Feeling nauseated from the news he just received, Vernon was at a loss for words and it took everything he had to muster up the word, "Okay," but he did then ended the call.

At that moment something in him changed and he got up from his seat, looked at Dana and said, "Rodney's dead. I have to go to the station and give a statement as well as identify the body and I'm not leaving you here without me."

Horrified, she jumped out of her seat and followed him. Vernon made sure he locked up the house before they got into the car and left.

"Call Eric's grandparents and make arrangements for him to stay there for a few days." She shook her head and did as he asked not understanding or believing all that had transpired that day.

Nate sat on the bed in his hotel room; his adrenaline pumping out of control.

"It served him right. Who did he think he was, following me? He deserved exactly what he got and anyone else who gets in the way will get the same thing! They thought they had me, but I showed them. Ain't nobody bad like me." He went on and on, rage taking over him. He knew that they would be looking for the car he had been driving. Especially since that cop was dead, but what they did not know was that he got rid of that car as soon as he killed him and got another one, so he still had the upper hand on them. All this trouble over a whore like Dana. He would make sure that when he finished with her no one would be able to identify her body or her dental records and that was a promise! He knew the streets would be hot right now, so he decided to sit tight a little while longer and plan his next move.

Vernon and Dana pulled into a parking spot at the police station, then she put her hand on his and looked over at him.

"You know we have to tell them all we know about everything that has happened. Too much has already transpired tonight, and I don't want nor do I need any more surprises. They'll be able to check my side of the story by bringing up the records in Georgia before I left and moved here." She stopped and turned to look him in his eyes. "No more secrets please, promise me. I don't know how much more of this I can handle. People are dying because of him."

He nodded at her.

"I promise from this day forward no more secrets."

He put her hand up to his lips and kissed it. "Let's go get this over and done with. Rodney never did liked dragging things out."

They got out of the car and went into the station. Vernon held her hand tight as they entered the station. There was a lot of hustle and bustle going on because of a cop killer on the loose. Vernon held her hand tight as he led her through the office. The scene was chaotic for her because the policemen were on edge for the reason that one of their own had been slain. Their only focus was finding this mysterious perpetrator before another one of their fellow partners was reported missing or dead.

They approached the desk, and Vernon asked for a Detective Mike Staples. The officer had just so happened to be approaching as Vernon was speaking with the other officer.

"Hey, Vernon, glad you could come to see me. Sorry for the circumstances. Rodney was a good man and an even better officer." The two men shook hands. "If you would follow me, I can take your statement."

Vernon interrupted the man before he could finish speaking. "Mike before we do this; Ms. Butler and I would like to speak to you in private please." The officer looked at the pair curiously before shaking his head to Vernon's request.

"Okay, follow me to my office," and the two did as he asked. With the three all settled in, it was Vernon that began with a recap of how it all started.

"About two months ago, I noticed a vehicle parked outside of Dana's house on several occasions. Every time the driver spotted me, he would drive off. But it was one time in particular that I noticed he had been completely out of the car and was walking towards her house, until he saw me approaching the house."

The officer listened thoughtfully as Vernon spoke, and then he replied "Okay. Then what happened?"

Vernon answered, "He jumped back in the car and took off. This made me apprehensive, so I stayed the night on the couch." The room was quiet as everyone listened, then Vernon continued. "Later on that night I heard noises coming from outside, but by the time I got out there no one was in sight. I went to the end of the driveway and looked up and down the street and saw nothing. When I turned back to go into the house, I saw a knife in Dana's tire with a note attached."

"What did it say?" the officer asked.

Vernon cleared his throat then went on.

"I am going to kill you whore."

Dana let out a loud gasp, her eyes wide as she looked at the man sitting next to her. Vernon reached in his pants pocket and took the note out of his wallet and handed it to his friend. The officer examined the couple's gestures as he listened to Vernon give an account of what led them in to speak with him. He nodded at Vernon to continue.

"Why didn't you call the police?"

"I did, that's when I called Rodney and explained everything and gave him the plates to run."

"That's how we found out the car was stolen, then it dawned on me to ask him to run the name of Dana's ex. It was just a hunch, but I wanted to be sure before I told her what was going on. Which brings us to tonight, Rodney called me the first time because he had found out that Dana's ex was not who he said he was. That he was actually the man who killed my ex-wife."

The officer let out a long drawn out whistle. He remembered the case and how controversial it was to Vernon.

"So, you are saying that this Nate Johnson is really none other than Brian Jackson? Vernon do you know how long we have been hunting him down? This man is wanted in the State of Georgia for breaking out of jail! Apparently, he had an affair with a correctional officer that resulted in her helping him to escape; needless to say, she won't be seeing daylight for a long time. There's also an all-out bulletin for his arrest for the murder of a Mrs. Helen Brown. Apparently, they were having an affair back in Atlanta. Her husband found her body with her throat slit from ear to ear just like Rodney."

Dana and Vernon looked at one another in complete surprise then back at the officer. Dana, realizing that he killed the other woman, thought about the run ins she had with her disrespecting her home, her marriage and most of all herself and shook her head.

"Rodney told me he was working on something and that he was going to need my help eventually," Vernon continued his story relieved that Rodney had covered their tracks keeping this from blowing up in their faces.

"Wrapping things up, that's how Rodney ended up dead and we ended up here." The officer looked over at Dana. "Okay Ms. Butler, what ended your relationship with your ex?"

Dana licked her lips then replied, "I was married to him; it was an abusive relationship to say the least. One that landed me in the hospital knocked unconscious; the police got involved when my doctor called them. They have a record along with pictures that they took of me and the state I was in at the time. That's what led to his arrest. They will have everything you need if you want to check it out."

The officer nodded at her, then looking at the both of them stated.

"In all my years as a cop I have never seen a case like this one and I have seen them all. The coincidence of it all or shall I say is it fate? Vernon, I need you to give me a statement, and Ms. Butler, God has sent you a guardian angel twice to protect you."

TWENTY-FIVE

Dana sat in the office waiting for the two men to return. They were gone so long that it seemed like hours. She was astonished at the sheer monstrosity of this situation. She did not know if she was coming or going at this point. To think that everything she had been through almost four years ago was not only a lie, but had almost cost her, her life. Not to mention the man she had been married to was not who he said he was.

Now he was back and threatening to finish the job he had started almost four years ago. Her nerves were on edge and she wondered if he would be caught before he succeeded at killing her. Dana heard the men talking outside of the office. She heard the officer telling Vernon that he would send a patrol car to police the area. He also told him that he would give him a call once an autopsy was done on Rodney to make sure nothing else had been done. It was about two a.m. when they were sitting back in the car, both of them exhausted and taken aback by the effect the day had on them, and their lives.

The ride back to Dana's was a quiet one. Both of them too tired to say anything and too disgusted to talk about it anymore. Dana laid her head back and closed her eyes trying to find some peace of mind. All she wanted to do was take another shower and go to bed. They turned on her street and passed by a patrol car making his rounds in the neighborhood.

They pulled up in her driveway and Vernon turned off the car, turned to her then asked, "Are you alright?"

She nodded her head without looking at him. He picked up her hand, put it to his lips and kissed it then they both got out of the car. He unlocked the door and they both entered with her going in first and then him. Dana looked around the room it seemed different now. Not as secure as it once did. Everything had changed now that she knew that there was a murderer on the loose and his next target was her.

Vernon walked over to the bar and poured two drinks of cognac, one for him and the other for her. She tossed back the dark liquid so fast that she felt its burn travel down to her stomach. Dana then turned and walked towards the stairs. "I'm going to take another shower."

Vernon said nothing but watched her leave. He then fixed himself another drink and walked to the refrigerator to find something easy to make. He remembered that neither one of them ate anything since they had been back earlier.

He thought about his friend Rodney and his relationship with Dana. So much had happened in one day he knew she would need time to bounce back from all of this. He promised himself he would be there with her and for her every step of the way.

Finding some eggs and cheese Vernon decided to fix them some omelets. It was late and it would be light enough on their stomachs to go to sleep on.

He was taking the items to the countertop when the power went out throughout the entire house. He called out to Dana but got no answer. Vernon cursed to himself and started feeling his way around the kitchen, going from drawer to drawer in hopes that he would find a flashlight. It was like finding a needle in a haystack. It was dark and he could not see anything in the room.

Dana was still in the shower when the lights went out and not being able to see anything she reached out and turned the water off. She then fumbled until she felt a towel that was hanging on the side of the glass door. She stepped out and before she knew it, she was falling on the floor. She had tripped over one of her house shoes. Getting back up she walked into her bedroom to find something to put on. The only light she had was coming from the window and she thought *something is better than nothing.* Nervous she walked over to her dresser drawers and got out a tee shirt and a pair of undies and put them on.

Vernon's adrenaline was pumping furiously as he searched for some form of light, when behind him he heard a noise his heart was racing, and he turned around. He could hear breathing, but because of the darkness of the room he could not see a thing. There was movement then suddenly a burning sensation in his ribs. He let out a gasp and he reached out his hands and grabbed the figure standing in front of him but the pain in his body was too great and he slumped to the floor.

Nate was standing over Vernon with a knife dripping with his blood listening to the other man's shallow breathing.

"How does it feel to have had two women sexed and killed by the same man? Did you actually think I was going to allow you to take my wife away from me without doing something about it?" Nate began kicking Vernon over and over until his breathing was no more. Vernon lay slumped on the kitchen floor. Nate then felt his way through the kitchen until he came to the entryway of the stairs. He began taking one at a time until he reached the top. He proceeded down the hallway until he came upon her room then he stopped. He saw the slender figure fumbling around in the dark as she put on her clothes.

"Babe what happened to the power? I was in the shower when all of a sudden everything went dark. There is a flashlight in the guestroom in the dresser drawer."

Dana noticed that with all the talking she was doing not once did Vernon respond to her. She walked towards the door saying Vernon's name when a hand reached out and grabbed her by the throat and threw her backwards across the room. Dana landed on the floor hitting her head on the edge of the dresser. She got up off the floor and ran to the nightstand, but Nate beat her there only to knock her back to the floor. Horrified and with nowhere to run, she fumbled to get up, but he punched her, knocking the wind out of her.

"I told you bitch what would happen if you ever tried to leave me. Now, I am going to kill you, but I want you to suffer first you stupid whore."

Dana, in tears now tried to think, too scared to say anything. She looked around the room. *Shit*, she thought. It was too dark. All she had was the little bit of light coming through the window and the only option she had was to try and fight him back in hopes of making a run downstairs to the front door. Suddenly, her thoughts switched to Vernon. *Where is he? Had Nate done something to him or worst of all, killed him?*

"God please help me!" she prayed frantically. *Let me get out of this alive and safe!"*

With nothing but the light from the window, Dana looked around for anything to help fight him back.

Dana was frantic and she knew she had to do something. She knew one thing was for sure and that was that someone was not making it out alive and it might be her. Fear took over as she spotted the lamp on the nightstand. All she had to do was reach for it and reach she did.

Nate saw what she was trying to do and got to it before she did. Dana got up and made a run for it. She had almost made it to the door when Nate caught her by the hair and yanked her backwards until she ended up on the bed. But Dana did a roll that landed herself on the floor again. Nate grabbed her by the leg and dragged her. Dana started

214

kicking him and yelling from the top of her lungs.

He let go of her and kicked her in the stomach until Dana gasped for air. He picked her up, threw her on the bed and began choking her. Clawing and punching him in his face, she could not breathe as she clawed at him, determined to fight him to the bitter end. All she could hear was Nate cursing her as he choked the life out of her. He had her body pinned to the bed, making it hard to move.

She felt her body go limp. She also felt something warm and a burning sensation course through her body.

There was a gunshot and Nate slumped over her before she saw him being pulled off her by Vernon. She also saw that he was bleeding. Everything else was a blur to her. She heard voices and shuffling all around the room and her chest felt as if it were being crushed. When she heard another voice saying, "Come on Miss breath please!"

What is happening to me? Why am I lying in a pool of blood? Why are all these people around me?"

Everything was hazy. She could not make anyone out. Where was Vernon?

"I have a heartbeat," she heard someone say.

"Take her to the ambulance and get her to the hospital now!"

Dana slipped out of consciousness.

"Lord please bring her back to me. I promise that I will do whatever it takes to spend the rest of my life with her, just tell me what you want. I love

her so much I can't take another day of seeing her like this and I can't live my life without her."

Vernon didn't leave Dana's side for one minute. Even when Julia and John suggested he go home, get some sleep and take a shower. They promised him that they would call him if anything changed with her condition. But he refused them both. Nate had tried to kill her and almost succeeded.

Dana had been laying in a hospital bed for four days. She had not responded to the doctors, to his touch, or his voice and he was not going anywhere until she did. He watched her day in and day out and even in this state she was beautiful. He thought about Eric and he had made sure he talked to him every day and reassured him that his mom would be just like new when she woke and recovered.

He might be young, but he was a very intelligent lad. Vernon made it very clear that he would be around for the rest of their lives and that he would do whatever it took to protect them.

He looked at the bandage around his own torso. That bastard stabbed him when he cut the lights. Luckily, it wasn't anything that stopped him from being there for the woman he loved. He wasn't going to lay in a hospital bed while Dana laid here alone. He felt like he was going out of his mind just watching her like this. *She has to wake up soon she has to*, he thought as he rubbed his fingers through his hair. He couldn't imagine life without her. She was everything to him. Everything and more.

He closed his eyes as he sat beside her, kissing

her hand. Picturing their future together and what it would be like when he married her, he whispered to her, "I will make it my life's work to give you a life full of love, respect and happiness. All you have to do is just wake up for me. I promise that you will never miss a day of smiling and laughter ever again."

He stayed like that all night long. When he opened his eyes and saw Dana watching him; he was so lost for words, all he could do was take her in his arms as he cried.

"Is it over?" she asked him.

Gazing into her eyes he answered, "Yes it's over, he is dead."

Dana did not know when the last time was she felt this relieved, and tears flowed freely from her eyes. She never had to worry about Nate Johnson or whatever his name was ever again. She put her arms around Vernon and noticed him wince with pain. Her eyes got wide with concern and his eyes soften when he noticed hers.

"Don't worry, everything is fine. I promise."

"Vernon, how long have I been here?" she asked.

He picked her hand up and put it to his mouth then he kissed it then he answered, "You've been here for a week."

Dana's eyes widened in horror, then he kissed her softly yet deeply on the lips.

THE BEGINNING

Before the ceremony, Vernon noticed his older son was not in attendance alongside him, so he asked his daughter if she had heard anything from her brother. She nodded then she answered.

"No, dad I have not talked to him since last night. He said he would be here. He must have made a stop first."

It was a beautiful day, the sun was shining, and the ocean never smelled more wonderful. Dana wore an exquisite ivory gown that fit her body nicely, accentuating every curve, her hair pulled back on one side and cascaded with curls that flowed past her shoulders. Her bouquet was of white roses and lilies. She was a vision of beauty.

Eric walked his mother down the aisle to the man that she would soon be married to. When Vernon saw her walking toward him with their son, he smiled at them. She was the most beautiful bride he had ever seen. He would be the best father he could be to Eric.

It was a private ceremony that consisted of eight people, which included the bride and groom, Eric, John, Julia, and Mr. and Mrs. Tate, Eric's grandparents.

Dana thought that she would never experience a love like the one she had with Vernon. It was one that she always wanted but never thought she'd have. Vernon gazed into her eyes as he said his vows and a tear ran down his face as he promised her that he would spend the rest of his life making her happier than she'd ever been. He slipped the ring on her finger.

"And now you may kiss your bride," the pastor told him.

"I love you Mrs. Cruze."

"I love you too Mr. Cruze."

Vernon kissed his wife.

THE FINALE

Downtown fifteen minutes away from the ceremony two men were talking in front of the St. John's River.

"Here's the money I promised you Mike. I don't know how you did it, but you pulled it off. What was it you gave me to make them think I was really dead?"

"Don't worry about it, I'll never tell," the other man responded. The two men looked at each other then smiled. "Well I guess I'll be on my way. I have a wedding to get to. Do you remember your ex-wife? The woman you just tried to kill?"

The other man sneered then nodded. Just then someone in a hoodie walked up and said, "This is for my mother. You do remember the woman you killed after you had sex with her?"

Before the man could say anything, the gun went off. The younger man just stood there watching the blood gush out of the dead man's head.

"Thanks Mike, I have been waiting for this a long time. He took away the only thing me and my brother and sister ever needed in our lives. Do you have the cinder blocks so we can dump this trash? We have a wedding to get to and I know my dad's wondering where I am about now."

"Go ahead kid, I'll clean this up. That's what I do best. This worthless piece of shit will never cause harm to anyone else.   I'll see you back at the reception."

"Thanks," is all he said. Then they parted ways.

Hello readers! Here's a little something extra for your book club. ENJOY!

1.) How many people did Nate kill?

2.) What was the other woman's name?

3.) Where did Nate and Dana go on their honeymoon?

4.) What was Vernon's ex-wife name?

5.) Where did Dana work? (business name)

6.) What was the smell Dana couldn't find?

7.) What was Dana's maiden name?

8.) Why did Nate kill Vernon's ex-wife?

9.) How many children did Vernon have?

10.) What was Vernon's friend's name?

BONUS QUESTIONS

How many prayers are in this book?

Who were Dana's bosses?

What hotel did Dana runaway to?

SYNOPSIS
Love, Limitations & Motives

A riveting tale about old love or the lack thereof and a true love found.

Dana is a woman who had to learn the hard way what love was not. When the real thing comes along, will the self-made promises of her heart interfere with the decisions of her present life?

As she comes face to face with a series of mysterious incidents and the man behind them, will her past collide with her future? Will it affect her chance for true happiness? Could this love withstand the test of time and the dangers that came along with it? Is this coincidence, or is it fate? Is love without limitations and motives?

Vernon Cruze is a man with a past. Life wasn't always easy for him, having raised his three children after the death of their mother. Now it was time to focus on his future. Then he meets Dana Butler, a woman with a past just as dark as his. Could the two of them get through the monstrosity of their past caused by one man or would the love they share cause limitations due to motives?

10866266R00125